WHERE SE̶ ̶ ̶ ̶ ̶ ̶ ̶ DARE

and other tales
from Herm Island

by Paul Sherman

To Anne,
With best wishes,
Paul Sherman
— x —
May 2018

**BLUE
ORMER**

2018

Published by Blue Ormer Publishing, 2018.
www.blueormer.co.uk

ISBN 978-0-9928791-9-8 (paperback)
ISBN 978-1-9998913-0-5 (e-book)

Book layout and cover design by Stephen Foote.
Photograph credits:
    front cover © Kevin Lajoie (www.aeriali.net);
    back cover © VisitGuernsey.

Printed by Short Run Press, Exeter.

'Where Seagulls Dare'
is dedicated to
Trudie
without whom I might
never have come to
Herm Island
in the first place.

CONTENTS

FOREWORD

Very occasionally, you are introduced to a subject that you know so well, but in a way that offers a unique and fresh perspective. This was very much the case for me with Paul Sherman's collection of short stories, all featuring wonderful locations on Herm Island.

There are a number of books featuring Herm, many of which are factual, and some of which are children's stories. Paul's collection of short stories offer adults a chance to step beyond their own imagination and visualise situations inspired by venues such as Shell Beach, the Common, St Tugual's Chapel and the Woodland Walk, to name but a few.

Paul had sent each story to me to read through as he finished them – each in a different genre, each encouraging me to re-look at a place that I know so well, which will also be the case for many readers. I am, however, almost a little envious of those who are discovering these locations for the very first time through Paul's storytelling. Either way, I'm sure that you will select your own personal favourite tale – I know what mine is!

I really hope that you enjoy the telling of these tales just as much as I do.

Jonathan Watson
former CEO, Herm Island

INTRODUCTION

The idea behind this book and its tales is for you to have as much fun reading it as I had writing it. The characters within the tales are entirely fictional although I have used one or two people's names at their own request – "please give me a mention in your Herm book."

The best suggestion I can offer you is to buy the book, then walk to each location on the island where that particular story is set and read it there. You will be in the right place for the right tale. The atmosphere will be apt. The brief introductions to the stories will guide you to the right place. Or if you prefer, just curl up in a chair and read them there.

On the other hand, if you have never visited Herm before, I believe that as a result of reading the book, you will want to come and visit this fantastic island for yourself, and explore the incredible locations in which the tales are set.

A lot of the tales feature magic and the supernatural. That is inevitable because Herm is a magical island and ghosts abound; it goes with the territory. But there are tales in other genres too – human drama, a war story, humour, adventure stories, even sci-fi.

My tales are a reverential tribute to Herm, borne out of my love for the island, my 'gift' to the island if you like, for all the pleasure it has afforded me over the years.

If you too are a lover of Herm, resident or visitor, I hope you take these stories in the spirit with which they were written. If you are new to Herm or even a stranger to it, I hope they will draw you into exploring this wonderful island further.

Not all the stories necessarily end happily. This is not a reflection on Herm Island; it means those particular tales lead to their natural conclusion and provide a satisfactory reading experience.

Neither have I made any of the staff or residents of Herm Island protagonists in the stories. One or two recognisable characters appear on the side lines which I feel helps to give the book a 'natural' feel for those living on the island. But all the main characters in the tales are completely the product of my own imagination, with a little help from sitting in the Mermaid Tavern courtyard and 'people-watching'.

Herm is a place of complete peace and tranquillity; those that live here and those that visit regularly will tell you so. And they are quite right. But the island's history shows an undercurrent of unrest, unease and other-worldliness. I believe it is right that these tales should reflect that aspect of Herm, albeit in an entertaining fashion.

You can still walk across the common at dusk, or visit St Tugual's, or have a late-night drink in the Monk's Bar in the Hotel. Or you can walk up through the Woodland Walk after dark and nothing will befall you. But as you do these things, if a little shudder passes through you, then my tales will have done their work.

Paul Sherman
February 2018

RETURN TO HERM ISLAND

As well as being the first story in this volume, it is also the first Herm tale I started, actually some years ago. However, the ending is comparatively recent. The climax to this tale is set on one of my favourite island spots, the North Beach (Moussonière), a wild and desolate but wonderful beach, where you can lose yourself and your thoughts. In terms of the title of this tale, I believe that once anybody ventures to Herm Island for the first time, they will always return. It does however provide a sort of introduction for the island if you've not been to Herm before. As you read it, I hope you will feel that you are coming home.

Boarding Aurigny Flight GR601 from Gatwick to Guernsey, Millicent Soames was a woman with a mission and the object of that mission was a glass jar inside a sellotaped brown paper bag, which she clutched fervently. A diminutive character, her grey hair tied back neatly in a bun, her tweed skirt and brown jacket rendered her almost invisible in a crowd.

That was the way Millicent preferred it – to be invisible; or at least, unnoticeable.

Neither would she rely on anybody's help. She was quite capable of reaching Herm Island on her own terms, thank you very much.

'I may be old but I'm not feeble', she often told her friends. So she had struggled through Gatwick Airport without the aid of the transport for those folk with mobility difficulties. A touch of arthritis and a gammy leg weren't going to interfere with her independence.

Millicent took her aisle seat, 6C. She tried to slip on her seat-belt beneath her precious bag. But wouldn't you just know it, she couldn't engage the two parts of the belt. Her fingers just weren't supple enough. Damn her arthritic joints.

One of the cabin crew, a tall girl with indifferent eyes and dark hair tied in a ponytail, noticed Millicent and bore down on her.

"Wouldn't that be better in the overhead locker?" the girl intoned nasally, "Then you'll be able to get your seat-belt on properly for us, won't you?"

"Oh no," protested Millicent, "I couldn't possibly. I mean…I can't part with this you know. It mustn't leave my sight for an instant. It's far too valuable."

The arrival of a second flight attendant, blonde and pretty, but equally of the opinion that the bag would be better in the overhead locker, resolved the situation. After a brief tussle and a few tears on Millicent's part, the object did indeed end up in the overhead locker; and the seat-belt was safely and securely fastened.

"It will be safe in there, won't it?" Millicent asked anxiously.

The blonde girl, who seemed kinder and more tolerant of older persons, stayed with Millicent for a bit, knelt by her, gave her hand a sympathetic squeeze and assured her unreservedly that her bag would be quite safe.

Millicent told herself that in spite of the fact that she had not flown for a long time and never on her own before, there was nothing to be afraid of. Yet, as the aeroplane gathered speed down the runway, she did close her eyes, hold her breath and grip the sides of the seat, as far as her hands would allow. Once in the air, she had to massage the fingers of both her hands, so tightly had she gripped.

The forty-five-minute flight went smoothly. Millicent enjoyed her glass of red wine and packet of cheese biscuits, although unscrewing the cap on the small bottle had proved a problem. The kind blonde girl had to come to the rescue again, much to Millicent's humiliation.

Touchdown on the runway at Guernsey was faultless.

Ignoring the behest of the brassy flight attendant over the PA, Millicent was out of her seat-belt, reaching up to the overhead locker before the indicator light had gone off. Alas, her miniscule form did not allow her to reach her prize; she had to turn to the girls for assistance.

She was totally oblivious to the scathing scowls of the dark-haired one but it was the blonde who pointed out that the aircraft had not come to rest and she shouldn't be out of her seat-belt yet. Millicent's pleading expression won the day and the precious bag was once again in her possession. She hugged it. With her eyes closed and her lips moving, she appeared to be praying.

Once outside the airport (the descent down the stairway and the trek into the terminal building had not been easy), a large white car bearing the motif 'Herm Island' was waiting. A grizzled driver with kind eyes stowed her suitcase in the boot. He reached for the brown bag, but Millicent clutched it to herself obsessively.

"I'll take this inside with me, if you don't mind," she said firmly.

"As you wish, ma'am," Grizzled Kind-Eyes said.

"It's very precious you know." She hugged it all the way down to the weighbridge on St Peter Port sea front, where the Trident ferry was waiting to take her on the twenty-minute crossing to the tiny idyllic island of Herm.

Millicent took in her surroundings. The Trident was

almost full; there were lots of families with hordes of children travelling to Herm for a day trip. They would be making for Belvoir Bay or Shell Beach to be sure. Maybe they would have lunch at the Mermaid Tavern.

Maybe *she* would have lunch at the Mermaid Tavern – it wasn't too far to toddle on her weary old legs. It was a nice sunny day and the Mermaid courtyard was a veritable suntrap.

Then tomorrow, armed with her jar inside her brown paper bag, she would set off from the White House Hotel and complete her mission. To the North Beach. To Moussonière.

She desperately hoped her legs would get her that far. No, Millicent, don't be defeatist. You have to get there. Failure is not an option.

Suddenly, she caught the eye of a man roughly about her own age, sitting across the way from her. He had a somewhat military bearing, sported an almost imperceptible moustache and in spite of his age, had a very alert expression and very bright blue eyes.

Those eyes seemed to be focussed directly on her.

He reminded Millicent of that actor with the sexy way of saying "Hello," Leslie Phillips, wasn't it? And the way he was staring at her in rather too much of a perky way, she thought, positively insolent. For a seventy-something year old man to be ogling a seventy-something year old lady in that provocative way was not right, not at all. Even if it was just a little flattering.

Yet there was something odd about the man. Although his interest in her was quite undisguised, he seemed nervy somehow, the way he kept glancing out of the window. His deep blue eyes, Millicent noticed, hovered between her and the walkway up to the quayside. Whenever they came back to rest upon her, she felt flustered, hot under the collar. It was disgraceful.

But they didn't stay on her for long. No, they darted back to the outside of the boat; as if he was watching for someone.

The engine started up. Millicent felt the Trident begin to pull away. The military gentleman suddenly produced a pair of binoculars, put them to his eyes and trained them on the shore. Only when they were clear of the harbour, did he put them in his hold-all and visibly relax, with an audible sigh of relief. Millicent wondered what on earth was up with the man.

Then he did something unforgivable.

He winked at her.

She turned away sharply, incensed at his precocity; it was all she could do to stop herself reprimanding him. But she did allow herself a peek back at him to see what his mood was now.

He was still ogling her, with that cheeky grin on his face.

Millicent turned away and concentrated on the view of Herm as the Trident ploughed its steady way across the water. The island was growing larger now and although it had been many years since she was last here, she had a warm feeling that she was coming home. She could make out the White House Hotel and Fisherman's Cottage and part of the South Cliffs. Yes, it felt definitely like coming home.

The Trident moored at Rosaire Steps, the tide being too low for the Harbour. The crowds alighted and the crew and island staff hauled the suitcases and bags destined for the White House Hotel and holiday cottages up the steps to the waiting trailer.

One of the island directors, on his way over to Guernsey, welcomed the new arrivals.

"Greetings old man," Millicent heard her unwanted admirer say, "Good to see you again."

"And you Major," the director responded. "Hope you're on your best behaviour this visit."

"Yes, of course. You know me, old man. Truth is, I've come to Herm for a little escape. Things getting a bit hot in the old metropolis across the water."

Then he glanced over his shoulder.

"But you know…" the Major said, nodding in Millicent's direction. "If you will put temptation in my way…"

He had lowered his voice now but she picked up some of what he said. "…dashing little filly…must find out her room number…".

Millicent couldn't believe her ears.

"Major," cautioned the director, "Best behaviour remember?"

The Major gave a lecherous chuckle and wandered off towards the Hotel. Millicent climbed the steps with her ubiquitous brown paper bag.

"Good morning Madam, welcome to Herm Island," came the warm greeting, "Is this your first visit?"

"Good heavens no." She panted a little, the effort of the climb taking its toll. "Admittedly, I haven't been here for some years, but when I was a teenage girl, my parents brought me over regularly. And then I used to come here with my late husband. I need to get to Moussonière first thing tomorrow morning."

"Well, we do have transport available if you need it."

"Certainly not. I'm no invalid you know."

She strode up the path, a small figure, head held high, bag clasped firmly in her arms. But oh, how her legs ached after the morning's travelling.

Small sustainable steps Millicent, she told herself, you're not as young as you used to be.

In the Hotel Conservatory restaurant that evening, Millicent discovered with some distaste, that the Major was on an adjacent table. What an uncouth man, Millicent thought. Yet he did look quite dashing. He was rather nattily dressed in navy blazer and light trousers, and his neck sported an expensive-looking cravat. And she had never seen such blue eyes.

Millicent, you're the one who needs to behave, she told herself, never mind the Major.

What on earth are you thinking?

It was during the soup course, that the Major winked at her again.

~

The following morning, Millicent was up early for breakfast and was gratified to notice that there was no sign of the Major.

The weather was not looking good. There were some big black clouds hovering ominously in the distance. If they delivered rain, her plan to get to Moussonière was in serious jeopardy.

Despondently, she pecked at her scrambled eggs and smoked salmon, whilst the faithful brown paper bag, standing solemnly on the table, kept her company.

By the time breakfast was over, the clouds had kept their promise and the island was drenched by heavy rain. Millicent stood in Reception, clutching her prize possession, looking out at the deluge. There was no way she could get to Moussonière in this. It was disastrous.

Then her thoughts brightened. She remembered how

changeable the weather could be on Herm. It would clear up by lunchtime. It had to. Millicent must fulfil her mission today.

She wandered into the lounge where a comfortable-looking settee opposite a roaring fire looked very welcoming. A sit-down by the fire and a hot chocolate sounded a very pleasant prospect indeed. And maybe a little nip of brandy? To warm her and give her fortitude for the coming task.

No sooner had she given her order to the waiter and ensconced herself by the fire, who should appear hovering over her but that irritating Major fellow. Today he looked like a retired sea-captain, with his naval-looking cap perched jauntily on his head, and his binoculars strung around his neck. First the rain putting a stop to her mission, and now this.

"Well met by firelight, proud Titania," he said in that lascivious voice. "Mind if I join you?"

"It's a public lounge," she stated flatly. There wasn't any point in saying no; he had already lowered himself into the chair next to the settee. Dear oh dear. All Millicent really wanted was to be left alone. Alone with her memories. To reflect on what she had to do. Her mission. Her hand went protectively towards the brown paper bag.

"I suppose an inquisitive chappie couldn't ask a delightful lady what she keeps in the bag?" the Major ventured, "Is it the family jewels?"

And then he once again committed the cardinal sin. He winked. That was three times in twenty-four hours. It was too much.

"I wish you wouldn't keep doing that," she snapped, unable to hold her peace any longer.

"Excuse me?" he said. "Oh, you mean my little

aberration, my inadvertent eye movement. Damned nuisance. I got that from a shell blast in…in…you know, I can't even remember now, so many terrible conflicts. Why can't people live in peace? No offence meant, I assure you. I suppose I should be grateful. To come out of the skirmish with just a twitch. Lots of others weren't so lucky."

Millicent felt a sudden sea-change in her feelings, and more than a tad of remorse. The Major hadn't been winking at her at all. He couldn't help it. It was a war wound. Her own father had been wounded in the second World War.

And suddenly, she wanted to pour her heart out to the Major. She had been too hard on him. Alright, so he'd called her a 'dashing little filly'. She should have taken it as a compliment. Millicent had to concede, she had been a dashing little filly in her time. Gilbert had certainly thought so. She patted the paper bag. Gilbert. He was here with her.

Maybe the Major would help her. She was sure he would. Anyone with eyes as blue as that couldn't be all bad. She turned to him urgently.

"It's Gilbert," she said.

"No, it's Ralph. Major Ralph Higginbotham, at your service," he said, giving a little salute.

"No, no, no. I mean the bag. My late husband. Gilbert. He always wanted to be scattered on Herm. On the North beach. Moussonière. I've had his ashes for years. Should have done this ages ago. I finally plucked up the courage."

"I see. That's why you guard the bag as if it was the Crown Jewels. Don't blame you. Like I said, I'm at your service. Anything I can do to help, I will."

"Thank you…Ralph," Millicent replied warmly, almost wishing he would wink at her again, even if it was an 'aberration'. "I'm Millicent. Millicent Soames."

Then, breaking the peace like an air-raid warning, his mobile phone started ringing.

He stood up to take the call. To say he was looking anxious was an understatement. Whatever had disturbed him? Millicent remembered back to the Trident yesterday…how his eyes had been scouring the harbour. Looking for someone. Looking…well…scared.

"Ralph?" she ventured, "Whatever's wrong?"

"Sorry," he murmured, gathering up his binoculars. "Need to check on the opposition." With that, he rushed out of the Hotel. Millicent caught sight of him through the window, his binoculars trained towards St Peter Port; a very haunted aspect had taken over his whole being. He came back into the Hotel, stopped at Reception, talking and nodding in Millicent's direction.

On his return, looking like a reprimanded schoolboy, he said:

"Sorry about that old girl. The enemy is nigh."

He looked so distraught that she could forget being referred to as 'old girl'.

"Listen, Millicent, if I may call you that," he said, "I have a little problem I need to sort out, but first, I want to get you to Moussonière so you can…do what you need to do. I took the liberty of ordering the Gator. They use it to transport people around the island, if…well, if they're not strong on their pins. It'll get as close to the Moussonière as possible, and then I'll get you on that beach, even if I have to carry you."

"Oh Ralph." Millicent fanned herself with her fingers, flustered. "I'm sure it won't come to that. But thank you. You've solved a big problem for me. I really appreciate it."

"Got to a get a move on though, old girl," he said, "The opposition is drawing in."

What on earth he meant by the opposition, Millicent had no idea. But he was certainly on edge. She didn't like to see him so agitated. She was beginning to warm to Major Ralph Higginbotham.

The Gator took them to the path that led over the stones to Moussonière. Ralph, the perfect gentleman, helped her down and they walked a few hundred yards, Millicent leaning gratefully on Ralph's arm.

The wind took Millicent's breath away.

Moussonière Beach is the wildest part of Herm Island. It comprises half a mile of isolated sand, rock and sea. There is a primitive quality in the way the waves crash and surge amongst the rocks and the way the wind whips the sand from the sand dunes stingingly across the beach. The mix of blue-black water and virgin white surf stretching as far as the eye can see down to Alderney Point and all in a constant state of flux, re-defines existence. The vast empty white beach, unpopulated apart from the gulls soaring overhead and the oyster-catchers chattering noisily at the shoreline, stretches in both directions, while the watchful eye of Pierre-Aux-Rats, the stone obelisk standing high on the sand dunes, stares down upon all.

It stared down upon Millicent Soames and Major Ralph Higginbotham standing at the sea's edge. It watched as Millicent sank into a sitting position on a rock, the walk along the beach having taken it out of her poor old legs. However, it wasn't a good move.

"What's up, old girl?" the Major asked anxiously. He must have sensed her discomfort.

"I'm not your old girl, Ralph, so please don't keep calling me that. It's just that…well…I don't think I chose a particularly dry rock."

"Wet your knickers, eh?" said Ralph.

"Don't be disgusting," Millicent replied. "Now, you hold the bag and I'll pull the jar out."

Ralph complied. He was left holding the bag whilst she withdrew the glass jar. It was tightly closed with a screw-cap lid.

"Bit like childbirth, if you ask me," Ralph commented.

"I'm not asking you Ralph," she said coldly.

Millicent was frantically clutching the jar under her left arm and trying to unscrew the lid with her right. Once again, the old arthritis was defeating her. Tears of frustration appeared in her eyes.

Ralph extended his hands and said gently: "Allow me," He had the lid unscrewed in no time.

"Why don't I hold the jar, and you dip your hand in and do your thing with the ashes," he suggested.

"Would you mind?" she said.

So with her ailing fingers, she took some of Gilbert's ashes out of the jar and cast them to the winds. But she was not able to raise her arms as high as she would have liked.

"It's no good," she said, on the point of tears again, "I don't want Gilbert to be cast on the sand. I want him aloft. I want him scattered high; to the four winds. I want to see his ashes fly!"

Her eyes were wide and excited now that she was actually here and accomplishing her mission; she felt a release that she had not felt in years.

"Steady on, old girl," Ralph said, "You'll do yourself a mischief."

"You must do it Ralph," she implored. "I'll hold the jar. You scatter Gilbert far and wide. As high over your head as possible. He wouldn't mind. You'd have got on very well with each other. Please Ralph, for your...for your...

dashing little filly?"

Ralph grinned and did the honours. And what an honour it was, Millicent thought, as Ralph took a handful of the grey powder in his large well-assured hands.

"High, Ralph, high!" Millicent called at the top of her thin reedy voice. Ralph hurled the ashes with all his might.

"Higher, Ralph, higher," Millicent urged shrilly.

Ralph obliged.

"To the four winds with you Gilbert," Millicent cried, "This is to celebrate your triumphant return to Herm Island."

Ralph flung some more with all the energy he could muster.

There remained little left in the jar. Mildred took it back and danced round in a circle emptying the final precious remains of Gilbert into the air.

Ralph, caught up in the joy of the ceremony, clapped his hands, danced a little two-step and called out in delight.

"Atta girl," he shouted, "You're giving your old man the send-off he deserves."

Just as Millicent was completing her final celebratory if tentative twirl, she noticed the two uniformed police officers standing on the sand dunes, about a hundred and fifty yards away.

"Ralph," she whispered urgently, "We have company."

"I know," he said solemnly, "They've been there about ten minutes. Didn't say anything. Didn't want to spoil the moment."

"What do they want?"

"Me!" he stated simply. "Oh, don't worry Millicent, it's all a stupid misunderstanding; some irregularities with a finance company I'm involved with. Nothing I can't sort out."

"You knew they were coming?"

"Of course! It was a friend of mine on the phone, warning me the police launch was on its way over. I rushed outside to check it out. But I also had time to arrange the Gator. Lucky eh?"

"And still you came with me? To help me? In spite of the fact that…how did you put it…the opposition was drawing in?"

"Yes," he said, "Couldn't leave a damsel in distress, could I? Anyway, wouldn't have missed the occasion for the world. Gilbert's send off. Stirring stuff."

"And you could have been…making your getaway," Millicent said dramatically.

Twenty-four hours ago, she loathed this man. Now, she couldn't stop the admiration glowing in her eyes. Her Prince Charming. Her Knight in Shining Armour.

One of the policemen held a loud hailer to his mouth.

"Major Ralph Higginbotham." The harsh metallic voice rang intrusively across the wild deserted beach. "Please make your way back to the main path. We'll join you there."

"You go Ralph. Do what you have to." Millicent sank down on her damp rock again. "I'll just hobble back to the Gator as best I can."

"Don't be daft, old girl," he said, "I told you I'd carry you, if needs be."

He stooped down, slipped one hand round Millicent's back, the other under her knees, and scooped her up.

"Ooh Ralph," she giggled, "You're so strong."

"And you're just a featherweight," he said.

He strode along Moussonière Beach with Millicent in his arms. She really did feel like a princess being rescued by a prince. Or a damsel being saved by a knight. The

24

thought made her giggle all the more. And she could have sworn the oyster-catchers and the gulls were all laughing along with her.

It was distressing at the harbour, seeing Ralph escorted off the island by the police.

"Don't worry old girl," he said, "It'll all be sorted out by tomorrow. I'll come back."

"I'll be here Ralph," she assured him. "I'll be waiting."

The officers helped him into the launch and he sat down, facing back towards the harbour. As they pulled away, Major Ralph Higginbotham looked up at her…and winked.

Millicent Soames took a big breath.

And winked back.

∼

THE LADY MARISSA

The Percée Rock, seen off the coast of Herm as the Trident approaches the Rosaire Steps, was reputedly where mermaids were once bought and sold. It's an attractive myth for a writer, too good to resist. The hole in that very rock is explained in this tale as is how the Mermaid Tavern got its name (all totally fictional). Add a sea captain adventurer, a mermaid in distress, a male witch, some cut-throat pirates and a dragon, and you have this story.

Approaching Herm Island through the fog was like sailing into the unknown.

As Captain George Stalwart steered his clipper 'The Freedom of the Seas' towards Rosaire, he was swallowed up by the low-lying intense miasma.

Wondering whether Herm was even there, it took all his seagoing skills to avoid colliding with the offshore boats.

George was surprised by the eerie quiet. The fog had rendered the atmosphere silent – no boat sounds prevailed; neither were there sailors' cries. Even the seagulls were mute.

Then George did hear something. Somebody singing.

A girl's voice.

Mesmeric and tantalising, the voice sang in a low vibrato.

George slowed the 'Freedom' down to listen to that entrancing song sung by an invisible girl in the Herm fog.

The plaintive refrain rang crystal-clear:

'To sing a siren song
Upon the Lorelei
There would I lie
And sing my siren song'

George had never heard such a beautiful sound. He had a fierce urge to see who was creating it.

Cruising towards the rock known to sailors as the Percée, George Stalwart beheld, seated there, the most exquisite beauty he had ever clapped eyes upon.

Her long yellow hair curled modestly over her naked torso, her eyes were ocean-blue, her skin milk-white. Beautiful as she was, her face betokened misery; her expression was that of a trapped creature.

George saw that chains held her prisoner; she was fastened securely to the stones of the Percée.

"What the deuce have we here?" George muttered, appalled that she should be cruelly exposed to the bitter winds that would blow from the Channel that night.

She continued to sing in her low mournful voice, unaware of his approach. He could not but notice her generous ruby lips, the fullness of her cheeks, albeit pale in the offshore breeze.

Had he not been so rapt, he might have seen the craft sculling up behind and the cut-throat figures watching him. Normally militant, George was under the spell of this woman's hypnotic singing. Her glazed eyes stared without seeing, as she intoned her haunting song.

George steadied the 'Freedom' against the Percée.

"What do they call you, fair maiden?" he cried, "How come you are tethered upon this desolate rock?"

Her eyes focussed upon him.

He had nearly drowned once, but it was nothing like

drowning in those fathomless eyes. He could stay drowned forever.

"Sailor!" she said, "I am named Marissa, after the seas from which I come."

Alarm entered her eyes. She grew rigid and tried to speak. She was staring behind him.

The blow to the back of George's head took his consciousness in a second.

As she reached forward upon the rock to warn him, she revealed part of herself he had not hitherto seen. Below the waist, she wore what looked like a green-patterned skirt which appeared to have been painted on, so tightly did it enfold her.

～

He came round, his head throbbing painfully as if a hundred bolts were emblazoned on it. Flashing lights impaired his vision and there was a dull rumble in his skull.

You dropped your guard, George Stalwart. With all your years of navigating dangerous waters, watching your rear-guard was your strength. You let it slip. Why? Because of a wench, albeit comely, but a wench notwithstanding. And they battered you from behind.

Fallible fool!

George's surroundings swam into focus in a reddish blur.

He was in a ship's cabin, chained. The scent of cedar-wood assailed his nostrils.

Another smell approaching. Brandy. A hand cupped the back of his head, not gently enough to stop him uttering a curse.

"Alright sir? Drink this!"

George sipped, the liquor restoring him.

"That's good," George murmured, the pain in his head mercifully dissipating.

He was looking into the eyes of a freckled honest-looking lad of about thirteen. The cabin-boy no doubt.

"George Stalwart." He offered his hand. "Thanks for the medication, boy. And your name?"

"Ben Clout, sir."

"Well then, Ben Clout, on what vessel am I imprisoned?"

"An evil vessel, sir. It would behove you well to escape. Few prisoners survive, be assured."

"A pirate vessel, Ben?"

"Yes sir."

"Would the captain be a certain Spanish Nobleman turned bad?"

"Correct sir. But as yet, he knows not you are here."

George shuddered. He knew what ship this was, and its accursed captain.

"The Crimson Valhalla," George whispered.

"Aye sir."

"Its Captain being Carlos the Claw." George's heart pounded.

"You know him?"

"Oh yes," George said, "We have clashed before."

"Then yours is the greater misfortune Sir," Ben said, "And more reason you should make your escape. Before he knows you're aboard."

George held up his chains and looked at Ben, who held up a brass key.

"I was set to guard you Sir. But I will set you free, asking one favour in return. That I escape with you."

"You'd risk your life for me, Ben?"

"Not just for you Sir. Life is bad on the Valhalla. She

attacked my old ship. I was taken by Carlos and his crew when she sank."

George thrust his wrists forward.

"Unchain me, Ben," he said, "We'll escape together."

~

"Where is the 'Freedom'? Where is my ship?"

George was impressed by Ben's strength as the boy pulled on the oars of the row-boat he had procured for their escape.

"Where you left her Sir. By the rock with the mermaid."

George stared at Ben in disbelief.

"The what?" George exclaimed, "Marissa…is a mermaid?"

"Indeed; for sale tomorrow. The Percée Rock is a well-known trading-place for mermaids."

"I don't believe in mermaids," George protested.

"You'd best start believing Sir," Ben said. "Because you were talking to one, due to be sold by traders Scrope and Fuzzle tomorrow. That was when Carlos' men took you."

"It was a girl in a green skirt."

"Bless you Sir, you're a caution. That was no skirt. That was her fish-half."

The row-boat approached the Percée Rock, but the 'Freedom of the Seas' had vanished.

"She's drifted away," Ben said.

"Stop rowing Ben, there's trouble ahead."

Marissa was not alone. Two dirty-looking vagabonds stood over her.

"Scrope and Fuzzle," Ben said, "Scrope is the short squat one. Fuzzle always has a string of slime hanging from his nostril. Never blows his nose."

"These are the rogues that seek to sell Marissa

tomorrow?"

"Aye Sir."

"They never shall, or my name is not George Stalwart. Let's take the traders now," George said boldly, "We are more than a match."

No sooner had he spoken than a suave sinister figure climbed sinuously onto the Rock. George recognised him immediately.

"Oh Lord," Ben Clout almost dropped oars. "'Tis my ex-master, Devil take him. He mustn't see us."

George watched his old adversary standing arrogantly, looking down at the victim. Carlos was dressed in a red velveteen coat, black breeches, expensive Italian white stockings and the characteristic tricorn pulled down archly over his eyes.

A large black claw extended from his left sleeve. Many pirate captains wore a hook.

Not Carlos. He wore the Claw off the beast that had claimed his hand. He addressed the traders, Marissa in abject misery at their feet.

George drew his sword, but Ben laid a restraining hand on his arm, as a number of Carlos' crew appeared.

"This is no time for spontaneous heroics," Ben advised, "Stealth is called for…if the intention is to rescue the lady. Let's find your ship."

~

The island was abuzz with activity. Ladies and Gentlemen of both high and low birth rubbed shoulders with pirates, smugglers and other assorted cut-throats.

George slipped into the Herm Island Tavern. The ladies were watching the men gaming and gambling. There was a jovial atmosphere. He ordered a beer and stood in the shadows, surveying the proceedings. Opposite, a group were playing cards – Scrope and Fuzzle, together with a third man. A crutch rested beside him. He was a little older than George and respectable-looking. An odd companion for rogues. The fourth chair was vacant, but a brandy glass was set in front of it; someone had recently sat there.

He edged forward to catch a better glimpse of the third card-player. Immediately, something sharp pressed into his back.

An oily Hispanic voice said in his ear:

"Stalwart! How delightful."

"Carlos," George said, silently cursing; caught with his guard down again. "The feeling isn't mutual."

Carlos gave a soft silvery laugh.

"I could kill you now," Carlos said, "But it would be messy in such convivial surroundings. Walk over to my colleagues and sit in my place. Otherwise I'll be forced to make the ladies scream at the sight of blood. Yours."

George obeyed. Scrope and Fuzzle didn't seem surprised to see him.

The other man offered his hand and said casually: "Captain Stalwart? Isaac Renfrew."

Shaking it, George wondered who in hell he was.

"I must return to my ship," Carlos said, "Leaving you in the care of these gentlemen. They'll welcome your participation in a game of *vingt et un*. Adios Captain. We will meet again. Soon."

George was puzzled. Why had he left him free? Carlos wanted him dead. George could handle Scrope and Fuzzle. And if Renfrew was crippled, he shouldn't be hard to subdue.

Fat Scrope wore a patch over one eye. Skinny Fuzzle did have slime hanging from his nostril. When he sniffed, it was like watching a yo-yo. Renfrew was a mystery. There was something about his eyes, one green, the other blue. They moved independently of each other.

"It's our heroic Cap'n," Fuzzle said, "Wants to rescue our Mermaid."

"Don't stand a chance!" Scrope said.

"Gentlemen," George announced calmly, "Tomorrow I will un-manacle the Lady Marissa, take her in my boat and return her to the Sea."

Scrope roared with laughter, his fat repulsive belly shaking with mirth. Fuzzle merely smiled.

"Let's drink to that, Cap'n," Scrope said, "Mr Fuzzle. Get him another beer."

"I'll get my own thanks."

That was when George realised he was in trouble. He found himself glued to the chair, unable to rise.

"What have you done to me?" he demanded.

"Oh, we ain't done nuffink, Cap'n," Fuzzle said, "It's all on account of our resident Herm witch here, Mr. Renfrew. He cast spells, he do."

George looked sharply at Renfrew. Still, he sat impassively, those eyes revolving, one green, one blue. That was why Carlos was happy to leave him. He had ordered George's bewitchment.

"I don't believe in witches," George said. Earlier that day, he hadn't believed in mermaids. Now he intended to rescue one.

George struggled on his chair. However hard he tried, he could not rise.

"Renfrew!" he said, "Is this your doing? Release me and I'll deal with these low-life scum."

"Even if you could move, Cap'n Stalwart," Scrope said, "Look behind you. A dozen of Carlos's men watchin' you, armed with muskets, daggers, cutlasses. You'd be cut down afore you reached the door."

"Mr Renfrew be doin' you a favour," said Fuzzle, "While you're stuck to that chair, you're alive. Right, Mr Scrope?"

"Indeed, Mr Fuzzle. So, we're going to play a little game of *vingt et un*. Stakes, Mr Fuzzle?"

"The Mermaid against your life, Cap'n Stalwart." Fuzzle leaned forward, the slimy plumb-line oscillating before George's eyes.

"Meaning…If I win, Marissa goes free?"

"Got it in one Cap'n," Scrope said, "If you lose, we turn you over to Carlos who'll do something nasty to your gizzard with that claw of his."

"Split you from nave to chaps," giggled Fuzzle.

"Hang your entrails from the yardarm."

"Yes, yes, I get the picture. Let's get on with the game."

It didn't take George long to realize that Scrope and Fuzzle were outrageous cheats and had no intention of letting him win. Every hand lost ticked away his life. Where was Ben? Couldn't he do something?

What about Renfrew? Was he really a Witch? He sat, looking disinterested, smoking a clay pipe.

Was another appeal worth a try?

"Renfrew!" he said, "Do you really want these blackguards to have me killed? To see that poor girl sold into slavery tomorrow?"

Renfrew, silent, continued to smoke.

Yet there was a subtle change in the atmosphere. George sensed something was happening. The very air seemed to vibrate. He looked at Scrope and Fuzzle, his vision blurred. Had they drugged his beer?

He couldn't move at all now. The room was spinning before his eyes.

Renfrew's voice came clearly through George's confusion.

"The odds are stacked against you, old man. Don't fight them. Save your energy. Dogs have their day – but not forever. Worms turn."

George didn't understand.

What was the man playing with? He was turning a glass bottle over in his hands.

Something was trapped inside. What was it? A mayfly?

Perhaps he shouldn't have come to Herm. It was the strangest little place – too full of secrets. He was a simple man. He couldn't be doing with all this…mysticism.

What happened next, George couldn't be sure. Ben Clout rushed in, waving something. A plant?

"Mr Renfrew!" he yelled. "I've found it."

"Ben!" George tried to say, but some spell had taken his tongue. How the deuce did Ben know Renfrew?

It all became a blur. Scrope and Fuzzle scrambled to their feet, their faces distorted. The Tavern was in uproar. Isaac Renfrew waved his crutch at Scrope and Fuzzle, who fell senseless to the floor.

George lost consciousness for the second time that day.

～

He awoke, not knowing where he was. A mermaid faced him. Not the Lady Marissa. Not as pretty.

"Captain?" Ben's voice. "Are you alright?"

George concentrated on the Mermaid's face.

A snap of Renfrew's fingers and George was wide awake. The Mermaid was a painting.

"Where am I?" he asked.

"Mermaid Cottage, my home," Renfrew told him, "I

saved you, Captain. Sorry for appearing unfriendly back there. Just keeping up appearances. Don't want Scrope and Fuzzle knowing whose side I'm on. Or that greasy Spaniard. I created the confusion so Ben and I could get you out."

"Is this true Ben?" George queried, confused.

"Mr Renfrew and I met earlier, Sir," Ben said, "He is also opposed to mermaid auctions. He paints mermaids."

Renfrew smiled.

"I'm an artist as well as a witch," he said, "Ah, you don't believe in witches, do you? Let's just say, I'm a man of many talents."

"Do they extend to rescuing mermaids?" George asked.

"Rarely!" Renfrew replied, closing his green eye and raising his blue one. "But I could help plan such an enterprise."

"And you Ben?"

"I am with you Sir," Ben pledged.

Renfrew produced wine and glasses and poured.

"Gentlemen, I give you a toast," he said, raising his glass, "To…the Percée Rock Redeemers."

~

So much for relying on the fog. The morning sky was cloudless, vision crystal-clear.

George cursed.

Renfrew appeared to read his thoughts. "Facilitating… fog." he said, raising his wooden crutch. Lo and behold, fog appeared.

Although the tall masts of the 'Crimson Valhalla' were visible, the 'Freedom' was hidden. Keeping their heads down, they scudded through the choppy blue-green waters towards the Percée.

"Remember Ben," George said, "When you hear me yell, fire the cannon. In the ensuing chaos, I'll get the girl off the Rock."

Ben assented, hand on heart.

"You're a good lad," George said, "When this is over, we'll cruise the world together."

"I'd like that," Ben affirmed.

"And me?" asked Renfrew.

"I don't see you as the sailing type, Isaac," George observed.

"No," he agreed, "I can't even swim."

"You welcome us when we come back," George said, "I get the feeling that anyone who visits Herm always returns."

He slid into the freezing-cold forbidding water and swam. Lesser men would have perished. George was made of sterner stuff. Besides, he was smeared all over with lard.

He found himself by the Rock, listening to Scrope and Fuzzle indulging their cruel trade. There were boats moored around the Rock, their owners doubtless bidding for Marissa.

George was to leap onto the Rock. On his shout, Ben would blast a shot from the Freedom's cannon to create a diversion; George would free Marissa using 'aqua-regia' on her chains. Renfrew had given him the brownish oily liquid in a phial, assuring him it would burn through anything.

George heaved himself up, sword drawn and instantly had Scrope and Fuzzle covered.

There was a sound of a hundred swords and cutlasses being drawn. There was no trading – just armed pirates, their weapons trained on him. A villainous lot they looked too.

The Lady Marissa was gone. The manacles lay empty.

An iron chain, its free end scraping against the rock, reached up through the veil of fog. It resembled the trick of an Indian Fakir.

"Where is she?"

Scrope pointed upwards.

"Bein' hoisted aboard the Valhalla. Captain Carlos is her proud owner. Bought her fair and square."

"You only have time to kill one of us before you're mincemeat," Fuzzle advised.

"BEN!" George hollered at the top of his voice.

There was a rattle of pirates preparing to pounce. It would take Ben five seconds to light the tinder and apply it to the cannon's fuse; another four for the flame to reach the powder.

"…seven…eight…nine…"

An explosion boomed; the cannonball screamed overhead.

"A bit low, Ben," George thought, feeling his hair part. The cannonball crashed through the Percée Rock, leaving a large hole. Scrope, Fuzzle and the pirates dropped down.

George leapt for the chain and climbed while his attackers came to their senses. It was cold and noiseless inside Renfrew's magic fog. He continued to climb, the rarefied air making breathing difficult. He had to keep going. The Lady Marissa was up there. Damned if he would abandon her now! Just as his lungs were at bursting-point, he emerged into clear blue sky.

The chain led up to a metal cage suspended from a gantry, presumably attached below to the 'Crimson Valhalla'. George must act fast if he was to rescue Marissa before she reached the Claw's clutches.

He drew level with the cage.

There she was, truly a Mermaid. What a resplendent creature! He gazed into her ocean-blue eyes briefly; too long and he might fall under her spell and lose his grip. Her green scales shimmered in the sunshine.

She looked up. "Sailor. You've returned."

"I've come to rescue you, Lady," he said.

George, hearing a sound below him, glanced down and saw a head emerging from the fog.

Fuzzle was crawling towards him, dagger between his teeth, murder in his eyes, the string of mucus dangling from his nose.

"We have company, Lady," George said, "A moment."

Clinging on with one arm, George produced the phial of aqua-regia from his pocket.

Two drops on the links below him and Goodbye Fuzzle. He uncorked the bottle with his teeth, the fumes stinging his eyes. He clung on with his legs, upside down, to apply the liquid.

Somebody else appeared through the fog.

Ben.

Damnation. If George severed the chain now, Ben would fall too.

"Ben!" he yelled, "Down. Quickly!"

Ben looked miserable.

"Can't Sir."

"Why not?"

"Scrope's behind me."

Sure enough, huffing and puffing, Scrope appeared, fat face glistening with sweat.

"Ben!" George cried, "I must think."

"Don't be too long Sir," Ben said, "Scrope is slashing at my ankles."

George acted. He threw half the phial's contents at

Fuzzle's face. Fuzzle gave an anguished howl, his hands going to his eyes. Having let go of the chain, his whole body upended itself and dropped, Fuzzle emitting a long high-pitched scream. The last thing George saw was his boots disappearing into the fog.

"Climb up, Ben!" George cried, "Take the phial. Burn the chain. Get rid of Scrope."

Scrope ceased slashing momentarily, horrified at the fate of his partner-in-crime. Ben grabbed the phial from George's outstretched hand.

"I can't do it, Sir," he said desperately, "It's not possible. I've an aversion to bein' upside down."

"Hurry for pity's sake. Scrope's recovered."

Indeed, he had. Dagger between his teeth, he was now scrambling nearer to Ben.

"He'll cut me Sir," Ben screamed.

"Do what I did," George shouted. "Throw the aqua-regia at him."

"Can't Sir."

"Why not?"

"I dropped the phial."

George uttered an expletive, hoping the Lady Marissa's vocabulary didn't extend that far.

Ben managed to squash his boot against Scrope's face stopping him using the knife, as he tried to prise Ben's foot away.

"Doesn't Renfrew have anything else up his sleeve?" George asked.

"Yes he does, only it's up my sleeve now. If I can reach it."

"What is it, Ben?"

Ben, hanging on for dear life with one hand, scrabbled in his breeches pocket. Scrope was slashing again, Ben

40

parrying against the slicing dagger with his foot.

He handed George the glass bottle Renfrew had in the Tavern, still containing some kind of winged insect.

"What the deuce do I do with this?" George demanded.

"You'll also need this." It was the plant Ben had found for Renfrew.

"More magic?"

"You ain't seen nothing yet. Get OFF!"

Ben planted a well-aimed kick at Scrope's face, who howled angrily, but still managed to hold on.

"You take one seed from the dragon-flower's head, squeeze it and put three drops of sap on the dragonfly."

George did it, not really believing in what he was doing.

"Then what?"

"You get a dragon!"

"I don't believe in dragons," George said.

However, the dragonfly, treated with sap, hovered as George watched sceptically.

A dragon? He'd met a mermaid, accepted. A supposed witch could perform tricks with his crutch. But a dragon? Never! Not one formed by squeezing sap on an insect.

Preposterous!

But something was happening to the dragonfly. It hovered in the air, its wings vibrating rapidly, making a humming noise. The dragonfly was now the size of a sparrow-hawk. Its eyes had grown and its colour was greeny-gold. Ben's eyes were wide. Scrope's face had a look of total incredulity. The thing, still growing, was now as big as an eagle, but with a wingspan twice the size; those wings were incredibly beautiful, reflecting all the colours of the spectrum. It had grown a massive tail, which lashed backwards and forwards impatiently. Its eyes were great blue crystalline orbs; in the centre of each, a large black pupil, surrounded by a vivid crimson iris.

Still it grew. It was now the size of a ship.

This was a Herm dragon, its scales as green as the grass that grew on the Common, its talons as grey as the stones strewn across the hillside, its eyes azure like the island waters.

Suddenly it roared and breathed fire and smoke. The smoke rose in the air, resembling the clouds that oftimes passed over Herm. Its roar reverberated through the air, a magnificent and terrible sound that would stir the sinews of a hero but make a villain tremble, which was just what Scrope was doing now.

The dragon roared again, tossed its head and emitted more pyrotechnics.

"Wow!" shouted Ben, "Go, dragon!"

And the dragon went. It spread its wings and took off in full flight around them.

People must have heard it all over the island. It circled, flapping its enormous wings and tail. Then it came for Scrope.

Hovering only feet away from him, it fixed him with its large eyes, gave another burst of fire which set fire to Scrope's boots and the seat of his pants. He screamed. The dragon executed its master-stroke.

To beat out the flames, Scrope had to let the chain go. It didn't occur to him that doing so would make him fall.

It occurred to the dragon however. As Scrope fell backwards, it flew underneath him and Scrope landed on its back. The dragon carried him away. Scope clung on looking like some gaucho on the back of a stallion.

"Bravo, dragon!" Ben called.

They climbed into the cage with the Lady Marissa – they were safe, but for how long? George sat facing the object of his obsession.

She smiled and he felt himself colouring up, his skin covered in goose-bumps. He gazed at her in admiration. Her human half was certainly pleasurable to admire. Those eyes!

He avoided direct eye contact because of his fear of losing control. To save her, he had to remain fully alert.

She said nothing – just sang softly, the amusement on her face making him feel distinctly uncomfortable.

Suddenly, a mechanical clank brought him to his senses. The cage shuddered in mid-air and then slowly began to descend.

"No guesses where we're heading, Ben."

"The last place I'd choose Sir," Ben said gloomily.

The cage dropped through the fog. They saw the 'Crimson Valhalla' coming up towards them.

Ben shrieked with terror.

The Claw stood arrogantly on deck, sword drawn, watching them. A mocking smile played about his lips. Behind him, stood a gang of his men, heavily armed. It was as if George was deliberately delivering Marissa directly into the pirates' clutches. He glanced at her face. It was etched with terror.

Arrival in the cage meant instant capture. If George fought Carlos, it would be like the card-game. Rigged!

There was one chance. The cage was ten foot above the deck. George drew his sword, launched himself feet first at Carlos and took him totally unaware.

Carlos fell flat on his back. His sword slid along the deck. The pirates couldn't take George. He was standing astride the prostrate Carlos, his sword at Carlos' throat, one foot on his chest, the other on his wrist to prevent him using his deadly claw.

The pirates shuffled a step closer, rattling their armoury.

"I wouldn't!" George pressed his sword against Carlos' neck.

"Stay back!" Carlos commanded. The pirate crew halted.

It was stalemate. George killing Carlos would lead to his massacre by the crew. Any attempted escape and Carlos would order his death. If he moved but an inch, that Claw, currently standing upright, could spear his kidneys, his neck, or worse.

Think of something, George!

He didn't have to.

A sudden commotion above them caused everybody to look up. A great shadow passed over them. A resounding roar ruptured the air and the smell of a sulfurous inferno hit their nostrils. The Herm Dragon cruised overhead, its wings causing a near-typhoon.

Scrope was still on its back. Not for long. The dragon tilted sideways, Scrope lost his grip and dropped, screaming.

His noise ceased, his face taking on a look of astonishment as he landed on top of Carlos, impaled on the claw. Carlos looked askance at Scrope, bemused. George was reminded of a music-hall act – a ventriloquist and his dummy.

Now to contend with the pirates! He needn't have worried. The dragon steamed in, spraying tattoos of fire at the Valhalla. The pirates leapt in the water to avoid being burned alive.

George ran to the cage…to the Lady.

"How do we, er…get you out?"

She laughed, a delicate bell-like sound. With amazing agility, she manoeuvred herself from the cage.

Inferno was raging all around them.

"Stalwart!" shouted a voice.

Renfrew was sailing 'The Freedom of the Seas' towards them.

"You said you couldn't sail," George called.

"I can't." Renfrew waved his crutch. "But Magic can."

~

The acrid smoke from the burning 'Valhalla' mixed with the Herm fog, causing an obnoxious smoggy stench. Renfrew dispelled it. With his crutch.

"Wouldn't a wand be easier?" George enquired.

They were sailing seawards for Marissa's safe return to the ocean.

Something was troubling George, although he had no idea what. He was steering the 'Freedom'. Ben slept. Marissa sang. Always, the Lady sang, her song in a major key; she was happy to be freed.

So, what was wrong?

It was Renfrew. George did not much like the way he was ogling Marissa. There was something bad about that look.

His blue eye was revolving independently of his green eye, an ominous sign. Renfrew was practising his 'art' – not painting – magic.

George's hands stuck to the tiller. He found himself glued to the seat. It was déjà vu.

Renfrew's spell!

The 'Freedom' shuddered to a halt, did a U-turn and started back towards Herm.

Concern clouded Marissa's beautiful eyes.

"Renfrew! What are you playing at?" George could still speak.

"Sorry Captain!" Renfrew said, "The Lady Marissa's mine. Can't be doing with portraits any more. Need the real thing. Don't worry. I've prepared a luxury cage. Semi-immersed in sea-water. She'll have all the comforts of marine life."

Marissa cried out in dismay.

"You helped me rescue her, man," George said in disgust. "Now you want to make her your slave?"

"You did all the work, Stalwart." Renfrew gave an ugly laugh. "I couldn't have handled the opposition myself."

"What about the dragon?" George said.

"He wouldn't work for me," Renfrew said, "My ideals aren't lofty enough. I don't use my magic well. He needs someone with morals, good intentions; someone who rights wrongs. You were he, Stalwart. You had to put the sap on the dragonfly. It worked like a dream. Remember, dogs have their day – but not forever. Worms turn."

"Curses on you, Renfrew," George spat, "You're as bad as the rest; a pathetic excuse for a man."

Renfrew's eyes ceased moving. "I'll release you once I have Marissa safe. I've nothing against you."

George scowled. Tried to move. Couldn't. Scowled again.

They were about to discover that Herm had its own Magic and had one last trick to play.

Renfrew hadn't reckoned on Marissa's vocal powers. Her song was in the minor key now, but louder, stronger. It filled the air. It echoed over the sea. It called Marissa's companions from near and far. The sea was suddenly full of mermaids. Suspended in the sea, their arms outstretched, hair flying, open-mouthed, all singing the most joyful song of freedom, their voices raised in unison. How their siren-song rang out. Its volume was almost painful on the ears yet wonderful at the same time.

Renfrew was affected badly. He put his hands to his ears, losing his crutch into the sea. Uttering a howl of painful anguish, he tried to stand, but fell overboard. The mermaids joined hands and splashed happily around him. He thrashed about, waving his arms.

"Stalwart!" he yelled, "Help me! I can't swim."

George's mobility returned. He woke Ben and together, they pulled Renfrew from the water. George looked out around the 'Freedom'. The Mermaids were gone and with them, the angelic marine chorus.

He looked for Marissa. She too had gone. She was safe at last.

Yet George felt an empty ache which he couldn't explain. He sailed the 'Freedom' back to Herm Harbour.

～

They helped Renfrew back to Mermaid cottage. With his crutch gone, so was his magic.

"I hear the Tavern is up for sale," he told them, "I may take it on. Put up one of my paintings outside. Re-name it the Mermaid."

"Do that," was George's parting shot. "Earn an honest living."

～

Ben and George walked from Mermaid Cottage to the Harbour, to re-join the 'Freedom'.

"Who's that", said George, peering at the bedraggled figure standing at the end of the harbour, sword drawn.

"Uh-oh!" Ben said and disappeared over the Harbour wall.

Carlos. A sad and sorry-looking Carlos, but Carlos

nonetheless. Mean and dangerous!

"Stalwart," he said between gritted teeth. "You took my Mermaid, my ship, my crew and my dignity. Now I am going to take your life."

"Oh dear," George sighed. "It just doesn't end, does it?"

He drew his sword.

"En garde!" he cried.

∾

THE SHELL SHRINE

This is the first of what I would loosely call the 'horror tales' in the book. Loosely, because there is no gratuitous horror – well, not to my mind, although I suppose others may disagree. Shell Beach is arguably Herm's main claim to fame. Surely, there cannot be many travellers looking beyond their front doors, who have not heard of it. A long expanse of sand stretching as far as the eye can see up to Alderney Point, is a shell collector's paradise, served by the gulf stream tide that brings fresh shells in every day. The hero in this story is a collector, obsessive to the point of stopping at nothing to protect his collection, and I mean…nothing!

"SHELL BEACH!"

Charles Stromberg shouted out the words in his sleep.

Edwina Stromberg, née Weitzschein, his wife, sat bolt upright in bed, startled out of her wits.

Charles' bony fingers crept out from under the bedclothes and started to sift through imaginary sand. Edwina relaxed, grunted in annoyance and lay down again.

"Shell Beach," he called out again, his body shuddering pleasurably, "Shell...lll Beach…ah!"

He elongated each syllable and ululated on the double 'l' at the end of the word 'Shell'. To complete the phrase, he finished off the word 'Beach' as 'Beach-ah!' Almost like a sneeze.

"CHARLES!" she yelled, sitting up again, "Vot are you doing? You scare me!" Edwina Stromberg, of Austrian parentage, born and bred in Vienna, spoke perfect English, except that she had never lost the habit of pronouncing words containing a 'w' with a 'v'.

"Dreaming," Charles said sleepily, "About shells."

"You are dreaming alvays." Edwina gave him a hefty dig in his ribs. "Even ven you are avake!"

"Sorry dear," Charles said, "It won't happen again."

"I hope not. If it does, I vill kick you out of bed."

Charles Stromberg, dedicated and committed conchologist, had come to Herm to enhance his vast collection even further, dragging the somewhat unwilling Edwina with him.

Shells! He loved their elegant shapes and colourful iridescence. Powerful emblems of sex, power, birth and death, they had been used for jewellery, currency, as magic amulets to ward off the evil eye; for marriage dowries, then to represent the womb, the generation of life. Finally, the dead had been laid to rest with cowrie shells over their eyes.

Shells, Charles intoned softly, as he drifted into sleep. He adored the feel of them.

They were his friends, the only real friends he had.

In sleep, his fingers still sifted through imaginary sand. He didn't even feel the next elbow-thrust that Edwina sent his way. Had he done so, he might have kicked *her* out of bed.

At breakfast the following morning, Charles was whispering to his boiled egg.

"Shell, Belvoir, Bear's, Fisherman's, Moussonière, the Hotel Beach," he said reverently, "A beach a day. On the seventh day, I shall rest from my labours."

"Vot are you chuntering on about, Charles?"

"Making my plans for the week, dear," he replied.

"Plans for the veek?" she snorted, "Ve know vot your plans are. You will be off all veek collecting your stupid shells."

"There are six beaches to visit. I was just running through them…Shell Beach, Fisherman's Beach…"

"Oh desist, quit, stop!" she protested, flapping her arms in the air, "You make me dizzy vith all your beaches."

"You are quite welcome to accompany me, Edwina," he invited.

"You know very vell I can't join you. My heart and my breathing problem vill not allow me to gallivant around any island, let alone this vun."

"So what is it to be then, my precious?" he asked, with gentle sarcasm, "A swim in the pool? Very cold, even at this time of the year, I believe. A spot of tennis?"

"Don't mock!" she chastised him. "I shall sit in the garden, read my novel and maybe venture as far as the Mermaid."

"Ah, the Mermaid. It didn't take you long to find the Mermaid, did it?"

"Vot's that supposed to mean?" she challenged.

But they both knew what it meant. Edwina's capacity for gin was as legendary as Charles' passion for shell-collecting.

"Don't drink the pub dry," he cautioned, "And no flirting with the barman."

Edwina Stromberg, in spite of her heart and respiratory problems, was an attractive woman. She turned heads wherever she went. And Charles was enamoured of her, adored her, went to all lengths to make her happy, but failed every time. Because his penchant always got in the way.

"Pah!" she said, and he knew that was the end of the conversation.

So whilst Charles was on his shell quest, Edwina ordered a large gin from the Monk's Bar and made her way to the hotel garden to find a recliner in the sun, with her book. At lunchtime, she teetered daintily on her heels to the Mermaid for a light lunch and another large gin.

When Charles returned to their hotel room with his cache, she was showering and looking forward to a cocktail whilst she prettied herself before dinner. Charles would be dispatched to the Monk's Bar to collect it.

Edwina stepped out of the shower to find him emptying a bag of shells into the sink.

"Isn't it enough that I put up with your mad hobby?" she raged quietly. Edwina had a remarkable way of raging quietly. To rage noisily would put too much strain on her heart. "But I draw the line at all your rubbish shells in the bathroom sink."

"I have to wash the sand out of them, dear," he explained, "I need to clean them. Get rid of the debris."

"Then clean them outside!" she said, "In the sea!"

Unperturbed, Charles carried on gently rinsing his spoils.

"I should have all your rubbish carted away," she said, "Ven you are out one day, I vill get the council to dispose of them all."

Charles took his hands carefully out of the water, dried them on a hotel towel, turned to her and said in slow measured tones: "If you were to even think about disposing of my collection, my dear, I would have to kill you."

He made his way out of the bathroom. She came after

him furiously.

"Vot did you say to me?" she said, "You vill kill me? How dare you?"

Charles chose not to respond. He had made his point. But Edwina wasn't finished. "You vouldn't kill me Charles. You couldn't kill me. You love me. You don't kill that vich you love."

"You're absolutely right. I wouldn't lay a finger on you." He smiled with a strange dangerous light in his eyes and added: "Unless you harmed my shells. Then you would force my hand."

Edwina stared at him, determined to outface him, to cower him, but the look in Charles' eye was sufficiently menacing. She dropped her eyes and turned away.

Nobody would ever harm his precious collection. Nobody.

Charles' week went like a dream and ended all too soon. Each day, he spent the whole day, from nine-thirty to five, filling plastic bags with shells, all shapes, sizes and colours. He was in his element, at one with the molluscs and crustaceans whose discarded exoskeletons he was accumulating with his usual obsessive fervour.

He even bought a large conch from the Gift Shop. It caught his eye and he fell in love with it. He picked it up, needing both hands. It was heavy. Edwina was scathing.

"Vot a vaste of money Charles," she chided him, "How are you going to get it home? Take it back. They vill give you a refund, I'm sure."

Charles took it back. But he didn't ask for a refund. He knew he would find a use for it one day. He paid for it to be shipped home.

47 Linden Close was a 'nice' house in a 'nice' little cul-de-sac and the neighbours were very 'nice'. Godfrey

Parminter lived at number 49 and Charles knew that Edwina thought he was very 'nice'. A nice house in a nice cul-de-sac with a nice neighbour. What more could Charles and Edwina Stromberg want?

Except that Charles detested, loathed, hated Godfrey Parminter. He resented the amount of time this 'nice' neighbour spent with Edwina. She was around there every five minutes having 'drinks'. He could hear them laughing through the wall. And when she returned to the house, she was even more critical of Charles than usual. Godfrey 'high-and-mighty' Parminter sowed ideas in her head.

Even on the day they returned from Herm, she just had to visit Godfrey.

When she came back, she complained bitterly about the tea-chests full of Charles' endeavours in the garage, which was why the car was always parked on the driveway of number 47, rather than in the aforesaid garage, which is where Edwina would have liked it to be.

"It lets us down," she said, "Other people's cars are in their garages. Vy not ours?"

Charles didn't tell her that soon the shells would be disappearing from the garage, because she wouldn't like his plan for their ultimate destination. No, she wouldn't like it at all.

Instead, he enquired in his unassuming way:

"Was this our neighbour's notion, dear? Did darling Godfrey put the idea into your pretty little head?"

"Godfrey is a man, Charles!"

"Meaning I'm not?" Charles' voice hid his bitterness, his long-standing suspicions about Edwina and Godfrey hardening like cement, in his mind.

Charles knew exactly what he wanted to do. To do it, he had to make sure Edwina was out of the house for at least a week. The tea-chests full of shells he had in the garage from his years of persistent and passionate collecting were to be used to turn the house into his own personal shell paradise.

So, it was most delightful and opportune when Edwina announced that she was returning to her native Austria for three weeks.

Three weeks to carry out the magic transformation of 47 Linden Close. As soon as she was out of the house and into the taxi for the airport, Charles got started.

He was still working two days before Edwina was due home. The tea-chests in the garage were now empty. Every single room of the house was adorned with shells. He was almost finished.

They were around the mirrors; on string chains hanging by the door in the porch.

They adorned the window-sills and mantelshelves, they were above pelmet and skirting board. They were across the bedhead, on the sideboard; they hung in festoons from every curtain in the house. They were along the side of the bath and on the telephone table in the hall.

The large conch, which had thankfully arrived after Edwina's departure had replaced her prize bonsai tree in the corner of the lounge.

But best of all on the dressing table in the bedroom, Charles had built his own special tribute to every crustacean and mollusc that had ever inhabited a shoreline. Forty tubes of superglue had gone into creating his masterpiece – the Shell Shrine.

Inside it, he had managed to fashion a seahorse shape out of his remaining shells, so the overall effect was very pleasing to Charles' eye. A seahorse fabricated out of shells jauntily strutting in its own shell grotto.

Charles was oblivious to the fact that it was so big, it obliterated the mirror in front of which Edwina was wont to sit and make herself up before their evenings out to dinner with acquaintances. With what careless abandon he had swept up her accoutrements of beauty, brushes and combs, bottles of scents and perfumes, eau-de-cologne, skin cream, toilet water, trays of eye make-up, mascara and rouge – all scooped up and consigned to the tea-chests.

Two days! Then Edwina would gaze upon his masterpiece, his magnum opus, his marine grotto adorned with a thousand and one shells.

As he was putting the finishing touches to his life's work, the doorbell rang.

It sounded irritatingly on the periphery of Charles's consciousness, but he didn't stop what he was doing – currently applying a thin line of superglue to a razor clam in order to affix it to another of his creations – a galleon made of shells to adorn the dining room table.

He had no interest in answering the door, absolutely no desire to know who was calling on him at…he glanced at his watch…ten to three on a Sunday afternoon. No, he wanted to be left alone. He was an artist. Artists should not be disturbed when working.

He heard the key in the latch. Not Edwina surely! She wasn't expected until Tuesday.

Charles held his breath. Who else had a key to his house? Had a burglar somehow got hold of one? Was he about to be mugged and robbed? He looked around for a weapon. His eyes fell on the conch in the corner.

Godfrey appeared in the doorway. Smarmy self-satisfied 'nice-neighbour' Godfrey. There was no trace of smarminess in his face at the moment however. He was gazing around the lounge at Charles' handiwork, transfixed at the sight. Charles was pleased at the effect his creation was having; more than he could have hoped for.

Godfrey let out a gasp of what Charles hoped was admiration, but was probably more of disbelief.

"Hell's bells," Godfrey said, "You certainly have been at work here. How long did all this take you Charlie?"

Another irritating habit of Godfrey's, calling him Charlie.

"It's my life's work," Charles told him.

"Evidently," Godfrey muttered.

Charles could see he was wondering what possessed a fully-grown man to devote so much to…shells? He would never understand.

"Edwina will go crazy when she sees what you've done to her house,"

"Her house?" queried Charles, "Godfrey, I built, paid for and bought this house. This is my house. And while we're on the subject, how come you were able to let yourself into my house?"

"Edwina gave me a key; asked me to check up on you. Just as well as I did. You had better dismantle all this crap before she gets back."

There is nothing like a direct approach, thought Charles.

"Godfrey, are you having an affair with Edwina?"

Godfrey's eyes narrowed. There was wry amusement behind the apparent indignation. He chose to ignore the question.

"Is the whole house like this Charlie?"

"The master-stroke is in the bedroom, Godfrey. I'll show you," Charles offered.

"Don't worry, I know where the bedroom is." He turned to the door. With that loaded statement, Godfrey

Parminter sealed his own fate.

The conch was just like the one the boys had in 'Lord of the Flies.' When you held it, you were empowered to speak. He always knew it would find a use. And its time had come. Charles felt empowered. Not to speak, but to dispatch interfering adulterous 'nice' neighbour Godfrey into the Afterworld with short sharp blows to the back of his head. With the conch.

~

Charles heard the taxi pull up outside. He sat in one of the plush armchairs and smoked a cigarette. He sipped the large Calvados he had poured himself and waited for the doorbell to ring. Outwardly, Charles felt calm apart from a slight tick in his right eye. Inside, there was a steady flow of adrenalin racing through him as he anticipated Edwina's reaction to his artwork.

Slam of car door. Slam of boot. Sound of suitcase on wheels rolling up to front door.

Voice of taxi driver thanking Edwina for tip. Edwina always tipped over-generously.

The doorbell.

Charles polished off his Calvados, took one long last drag of his cigarette and then crushed it out on the ormer shell he kept expressly for the purpose.

He levered himself out of the chair and in a studied unhurried fashion, he moved into the hall to the front door and opened it.

Not even in the house yet and already Edwina was fuming.

"I might have known you vouldn't come out to velcome me," she snapped, "And to add insult to injury, you keep me vaiting on the doorstep."

"Please come in my dear," he said with a forced smile on his lips. "Welcome home. I've made a few changes. I hope you approve."

She wouldn't. Quite the opposite, in fact. It was the calm before the storm. But he was pleasantly anticipating the storm.

Edwina stepped in. Charles made no attempt to pick up her suitcase.

"Charles!" she said, sniffing the air like a mongoose on its hind legs, "You have been smoking."

"Yes dear," he said, "And I intend to carry on doing so."

"Ve vill see about that," she said, her look as venomous as a cobra's bite.

"I said I'd made a few changes, Edwina. There are going to be quite a few changes around here. Why don't you go into the lounge, put your feet up and I'll bring you a gargantuan gin and tonic."

Edwina, encouraged by the thought at least, stepped into the shell-adorned lounge, totally unprepared for what she was about to see. And stopped. And stared. And let out a howl of anguish.

"Charles! Vot have you done?" she yelled, "Vere are all my pretty things? My ornaments. My treasures. Charles, have you lost your mind?"

"No dear, but you are about to lose yours."

She stared around the room, open-mouthed, like a trapped rabbit, now unable to utter anything except a short sharp series of shrill shrieks. She sounded like Morse Code on speed.

Charles had done a thorough job and was proud of it. After three weeks of shells and superglue, he was so proud of his masterpiece, and he was delighted to see the effect it had on Edwina. It was a pleasurable build up to what was to come. She had yet to see the kitchen, the dining room, the bathroom and finally…the bedroom.

By the time Charles led her upstairs, she was sobbing uncontrollably, each sob sticking in her throat and obviously causing her pain. She would feel better when she saw his *pièce de resistance*, which was waiting for her on the dressing table and over which, he had taken so much care. He couldn't wait to see her face.

"Come along my dear," he said, guiding her by the elbow through the doorway into their bedroom. "Someone you know intimately is waiting for you."

"Vot do you mean, Charles?" she managed to stutter out between sobs, "Who vould be in our bedroom?"

"Well don't say you're surprised dear," he said, "While you were away, I discovered that he knew exactly how to get to the bedroom."

"Charles, sometimes I think you are going crazy," Edwina said, seeming to have regained some of her composure.

The bedroom itself might have been the final straw for Edwina. But the actual final straw was sitting on the dressing-table.

Charles had removed the sea-horse and replaced it with something far more choice, much more apposite.

Godfrey's head.

A razor clam shell was inserted sideways in his mouth giving him a permanent toothless rictus. Out of his nostrils – whirly pointed shells and stuck to the sides of his head, ormer shells in place of his ears. And where his eyes should have been, two cowrie shells.

Charles stood behind Edwina, conch at the ready. But he didn't have to use it.

With one final agonized choking rattle in her throat,

Edwina beat her chest with her hands and dropped to the floor. She convulsed a few times and then lay still.

Charles sighed and placed the conch on the bed, sitting himself beside it gazing at the shell shrine. He took a shell out of his pocket and held it to his ear. Joy of joys, the sound of the sea pounding the shoreline of Shell Beach assailed his ears. His eyes misted over with salt tears of ecstasy.

Already he was planning the extension to his shell tableau. But he obviously needed to enlarge it, to make room for Edwina. For that, he would need to enlarge his collection. It was time to book himself another trip to Herm. More shells were needed. He had to get back to Shell Beach.

BENEATH EACH BLUEBELL

The woodland path was created on Herm comparatively recently and the island gardeners have made a truly spectacular walk running down almost parallel to the driveway. At the bottom is a quiet glade, complete with a gazebo and pond. In the Spring, the bluebells are manifest and very beautiful. A great setting for a story, of course. Particularly if the haiku is true:

> *Beneath each bluebell*
> *There lies a sleeping fairy*
> *Please watch where you tread.*

The 'villain' of this story didn't watch where he trod – and paid the price – just as any potential enemy of Herm Island should do.

How was it possible to get so irritated at the sight of someone's jawline?

Claire felt very irritated. And it was the profile of her fiancé Ian Fensham that was making her feel that way.

She hated the way he was staring greedily at Herm Island as the Trident approached the harbour. She knew what was going through his head. And she loathed him for it.

She detested him full stop. It was time to call off the engagement. She'd known the time would come.

Marry a rich man, her mother had said. Ian was definitely rich, no doubt about that.

She had tolerated rather than loved him.

Claire Graham wasn't even sure what she had ever seen in him. They had been thrown together in a night club, found some sort of mutual attraction and formed a relationship.

Now it was time to end it.

As the Trident ploughed nearer and nearer to Herm, Claire did not get the usual feelings of excitement stirring inside her. It was a mistake bringing Ian here.

His hairline was too near his eyes and his chin jutted out in a sort of Neanderthal way. It was as if his features had developed alongside his lofty ambitions. At school, he didn't do very well academically, except when wrangling for various other students' property that he fancied; for instance, a particularly fancy fountain pen or a comic book and on one occasion, a mobile phone. He felt he had accumulated his spoils honestly by square dealing. The owners deprived of their prizes might have disagreed. Ian Fensham 'the profiteering pillock' as he became known, left school with no qualifications but plenty of business acumen.

At the age of eighteen, he'd 'bought' a taxi firm for the sum of twenty pounds.

They had reached Herm Harbour.

~

It took Ian just an hour and thirty minutes to scour Herm. He strode in front of Claire like royalty as they circumnavigated the island. His Neanderthal eyes took in every feature. Claire could almost see the dollar signs in his eyes. When they passed the White House Hotel, he stopped, his hands on his hips, sighed, tutted and shook his head.

On the common, he took in the view in a broad sweep.

"Golf course…definitely," she heard him say almost under his breath, "What's that place over there?" he asked, as they descended the steps from the South Cliff.

"That's Jethou," Claire told him, "A privately owned island."

Claire could see his shifty eyes sizing up impossible possibilities.

By the time they got to the Mermaid Tavern for lunch, Claire sensed that Ian had made his own inventory of the 'improvements' he would make to Herm if he had half a chance. May he never get it!

Ian was never short of conversation. It didn't take him long to become the centre of attention in the Mermaid. Claire sat in the corner with a glass of wine, her empty plate in front of her; she didn't really want to be associated with him. She was just waiting for the opportunity to tell him their engagement was off.

How would he take it, she wondered? Was there a way of 'letting him down' gently?

"The trouble with Herm is…"

Oh no, he was about to start. This was going to be embarrassing.

The assembled company waited to find out what Ian thought the trouble with Herm was. Most of them already had looks of disdain on their faces. It was clear what the bar staff thought of Ian. Their knowing glances at each other said it all.

Maybe I don't want to let him down gently, Claire thought. He needs to come down hard.

"Herm has no forward thinking, no ambition, no enterprise," he was saying. "I mean, the White House Hotel is all very well, but what about a second more glitzy hotel? On Shell Beach."

There was silence in the bar.

"And that common. It's a big waste of space. I'd put a golf course there. Build a bar and club house. Maybe a ballroom."

Claire closed her eyes and wished the floor would open up and swallow him whole, so that she would never have to see him again. Never have to endure listening to his crazed ambitious plans.

"Rip down the tennis courts and build a casino," Ian was saying, "And that Radziwell's walk. Too steep. Nice at the top but who would venture up there? Now...what about a funicular railway to get you to the top?"

He looked round, the expression on his face proclaiming that he was wondering why the hell nobody had thought of it before.

"And you've got to have a helipad!" He was almost into shouting mode now. That was his way; when he got excited, his voice increased in decibels.

"I mean...the Trident," he scoffed, "Every time a gale blows, it's cancelled. Let's invent the Heli-Trident. Not just five times a day! A continuous service. With a land train to get people to the hotels. They wouldn't have to walk round the island any more. We'll create an infrastructure that allows them to ride round it." His eyes widened. "Hey! What about a monorail?"

He paused and looked around him at the astounded audience he had commanded. Claire knew him so well. He imagined he was impressing them. If only he could read their faces a little better, he might know what was going on in their minds.

"We'll buy Jethou," he proclaimed, "Put a hotel there as well. Create a causeway between the islands. No, a bridge.

No! Better still, a chairlift. Then we could create a dry ski slope there."

Claire could stand it no longer. Unseen, she slipped out of the Mermaid just as Ian was saying:

"A night club. That's another thing Herm could do with. Bars, dance floor, disco, a decent restaurant. Why, we could rip the Mermaid down and build it here. Then we could create a decent holiday village up the top there, where the Manor House is. Chalets surrounding a heated indoor swimming pool..."

~

She was angry. No, she was incensed, fuming; appalled that Ian could make such a fool of himself in front of so many people, most of whom she knew.

It had to be tonight. She would tell him the engagement was off as soon as he got back to the cottage.

But she didn't. Because he came in drunk. Four sheets to the wind! She knew that trying to tell Ian anything when he was in that state was pointless. Too many pints of Herm Gold in the Mermaid! Probably a few chasers as well. Claire wouldn't be surprised if he hadn't been bought drinks, just to shut him up.

He would never be able to engage with any truth, however brutal.

"Hello doll!" he said as he lurched into the cottage, almost knocking the door off its hinges...

Doll! DOLL?

How dare he call her doll?

There wasn't anything he could do anymore that would mollify or placate her or induce in her any feelings of warmth or liking towards him. This was it!

He collapsed in the chair and started fiddling with his

camera.

"Got some great photo'sh of the island," he said. "Real cool! Get s'more tomorrow."

She couldn't bear to be in his company a moment longer. She grabbed her coat and walked out without a word.

"Hey, where you off to now?" Ian demanded. She heard him continuing to shout after her but missed what he said, because by this time, she had slammed the door angrily after her.

It was dusk on Herm and a beautiful time of the day. The moon was already full and the lights of Guernsey twinkled tantalisingly across the water.

What to do? What to do? She just didn't want to go back to his company. From Sea Holly, she reached the path that led to the woodland walk and suddenly wondered what the bluebells there would look like at dusk.

They were always impressive but she had never seen them at this time before. She turned along the path, aware that it was a mystical time of evening. There was a sweet spring fragrance in the air, and even now, there were still some late birds singing their eulogies to the demise of the day.

The air was a little chill as she walked along the path to the top of the woodland steps.

Pulling her jacket around her, she heard a foghorn sounding out from across the channel.

She reached the top of the walk and looked down. She gasped at the splendour she was viewing. The spectacle of bluebells to either side of the path was such a breathtaking sight.

The evening light of dusk caught them beautifully – an undulating sea of blue carpet stretching beneath her.

Yes. She might walk down that pathway to the little gazebo in the glade and imagine she was a very special visitor to the island – not a red carpet, but a very deep blue one.

She knew she would be safe. You were always safe on Herm. There was no danger here. At least, not from humans.

Why on earth had that thought come into her mind?

Her mind flicked back to Ian's outrageous tirade in the Mermaid. Herm can't hurt you Ian, but you could hurt Herm. With your expansionist ideas and money-motivated drive, you could be a danger to Herm. A real danger.

There was a tinkling sound. The air grew warmer. A breeze caressed her face, almost as if someone who loved her had stroked her cheek.

The bluebells; something was happening to the bluebells. They were moving. No, not possible. Phototropism only makes plants move when the sun is shining…and not that fast.

Suddenly for no reason, her heart had increased in speed. It was racing.

And suddenly…suddenly…the whole carpet of bluebells lit up. Each individual bluebell seemed to be fitted with an LED.

Gently, very gently, the petals of the bluebells lifted to reveal – what?

She wasn't sure.

Certainly, something had happened to the bluebells. They seemed to be animated.

They were dancing. There was no music, except for the Herm wind sighing through the trees, although that was music in itself. The Herm symphony.

It played every hour of the day; it was just that the instrumentation changed. Now it was soothing and mellow – and the bluebells moved in time with it.

But there was something else. There was something beneath each bluebell. She had once read a haiku:

Beneath each bluebell
There lies a sleeping fairy
Please watch where you tread

But the fairies here weren't sleeping. They were wide awake. They were glittering and dancing in the evening breeze. They were extending tiny welcoming hands to her. They were dressed in sparkling white tutus and tunics; they carried tiny jewelled wands and their eyes were big, bright green and inquisitive.

And those eyes were all watching her.

"Hello," she said hesitantly.

It might have been gentle laughter on a Nano-scale magnified a million times. It might have been ten thousand fairy voices raised in song on the Herm evening air. It might have been a unanimous greeting from the bluebell fairy folk, but a sudden symphony of tiny bells ringing fortissimo and allegro burst upon the air. The fairies were dancing but they were also waving and they were obviously noisy and excited. They were returning her 'hello'. The whole woodland walk was ablaze with beautiful blue light. The whole air was filled with the exquisite sound of miniature tintinnabulation.

"Hello," she said again, and as she greeted the fairies a fantastic feeling of warmth spread through her. All thoughts of Ian and his grasping greed were forgotten. If it was his avarice that had infuriated her and driven her out into the wood at night, then he had done her a favour. How could she ever have missed this amazing sparkling spectacle?

They seemed to be beckoning her. To a fairy, they were leaning forward as if extending her a welcome. She could see their little enthusiastic faces leaning up towards her, expectant, enthusiastic, energised with welcoming love.

"You want me to dance with you?" she said breathlessly.

> *Beneath each bluebell*
> *There lies a sleeping fairy*
> *Please watch where you tread*

She would definitely need to watch where she trod. The thought of standing on any of these delicate fragile creatures filled her with dread. They were out from underneath the bluebells and they were there for her. She was their guest of honour.

She felt like a princess as she descended the steps of the woodland walk. As she walked through her parade of honour, they turned and watched her, glittering and making their incredible music as she went.

They made way for her. As she walked across the carpet of blue, they moved aside in a sweeping motion to provide a pathway for her.

Then the unthinkable happened.

"Claire!"

Ian's voice rang out through the evening air. He had come after her.

The drunken Elf-King had arrived!

For a moment, the fairy folk stopped their music. For seconds, there was a silence broken only by the rustling of the trees. The carpet of bluebell folk turned to the newcomer.

"Hide!" Claire whispered to them as loud as she dared. "Go back under your bluebells. Hide yourselves!"

But they appeared not to hear or understand. Rather they seemed to want to welcome another visitor to their woodland world. They began their iridescent music all over again, this time facing away from her and applauding and welcoming Ian Fensham, who was careering drunkenly down the path not able to take care with where he was putting his feet, as he clicked away with his digital camera.

"Ian. Don't photograph them. You mustn't!" she cried out.

"But this is fantashtic," he said, as he stopped to check the photos he had taken. "Thank you for walking out on me Claire. You've stumbled on a gold mine. Think of the commercial possibilities here. A guided evening walk to see the fireflies and glow-worms."

"Fireflies..." Claire started to say, and stopped. Good. Let him think that. Let him not realise the truth. He will bring harm to these precious people. Everything he touches turns into nothing but money. And all the evil that brings. She didn't want him to become a Herm Midas!

The precious folk in the meantime, had an agenda of their own. They seemed to be in debate. There was an urgent flurry occupying them now. First, they turned their bluebell heads one way towards Claire and then in the other direction towards Ian. They were perturbed, undecided. There was an undercurrent to their music, a concern they felt that all was not well. Maybe they felt Claire's concern about this new visitor who appeared to like to shout rather than whisper. Who had not returned their greeting. Who was unfriendly.

"Why shouldn't I photograph them?" Ian yelled,

pointing his camera this way and that and clicking like there were no tomorrows.

It was when he used his zoom to get some close-ups that he suddenly stopped, slowly lowered his camera and said in a slow deliberate voice:

"Claire. Whatever these things are, they've got faces." As if to confirm, he looked at his screen again and gasped in amazement.

"I'm seeing an old man's face on one of those things," he said, "And there are young girls, and young men, and children, and they've all got…I don't…I can't believe this…they've all got…wings. Tiny wings. THEY'VE GOT WINGS CLAIRE!"

His shout caused another tremor of alarm to go through the fairy folk. It was as if the bluebells were doing a Mexican wave. But the tiny tinkling sound had reached a volume now of immense proportion. Claire thought that they were undergoing the most heated debate that they had ever experienced in all their fairy lives. It was as if they knew they were facing a calamity and that they were having a war council to decide how to deal with it.

Ian looked at Claire accusingly. He appeared now to be absolutely sober.

"You weren't going to tell me, were you? You didn't want me to know. You wanted me to think they were glow-worms. And fireflies. How could you want to keep this to yourself Claire? Can't you see the commercial possibilities?"

He moved a few more steps down the woodland walk towards her.

"TWILIGHT TOUR ALONG THE WOODLAND WALK TO SEE THE HERM FAIRIES!" he proclaimed. "Good grief! We'll make a fortune."

He twisted around to take a photograph of the blue silvery hordes behind him. And in doing so, he made a grave mistake. His foot left the path and trod on the bluebell covered grass.

A high-pitched tiny scream rent the air.

"Ian!" Claire cried out despairingly, "How could you? You've trodden on one of them."

Beneath each bluebell...

Now the fairies knew. Now they realised that the one called Ian was their enemy. Not like the gentle Claire, with the kindly smiling face and loving manner. One telepathic thought travelled like wave motion through the minds of the fairies.

DEAL WITH THE ENEMY!

They didn't have to talk about it. They seemed to know just what to do. It was as if they had emergency procedures in place.

Suddenly, Ian was horizontal. They had upended him. But he was moving. The bluebells were carrying him down the slope towards the glade in a sort of peristaltic action. If he hadn't looked so scared, he might have resembled a rock singer being carried out over the mosh pit by the hands of adoring fans. These were not adoring fans.

"Claire," he screamed, "Help me!"

But Claire had another agenda. She felt an overwhelming desire to laugh. It would infuriate Ian, she knew. She tried to hold it in. Then she realised it wasn't the bluebells propelling Ian down the slope; it was the fairies with their little hands extended, but using the bluebells.

At the bottom of the slope was a pond. A warning sign read 'Danger! Deep Water!' and it was covered with green algae.

"HELP!" Ian yelled, "HELP ME! CLAIRE!"

But he continued his descent down the woodland path, surely and smoothly, as the flotilla of fairy folk, as swift as a bobsleigh, slid their unwilling passenger towards his final destination. Even if Claire had wanted to help him, there was nothing she could do. The bluebell fairies had a mission and who was she to stop them?

There were her friends. They liked her. They had made her feel special. And if your friends want to do something they really want to do, you don't stop them, do you?

Of course you don't.

The drunken Elf-King's barge was now at the bottom of the walk and heading towards the hidden depths. Claire strained her ears. Was she hearing things? No, she wasn't. The fairies were singing an anthem. Their little voices were raised in triumph. It was a celebration.

There was a colossal splash.

The Proud Parade had precipitated the Profiteering Pillock in the pond.

Ian splashed about, raved and ranted and flailed with his arms to stay afloat, his face covered in green weed.

The fairies were hysterical with laughter as they made their way backwards up the steps to their protective bluebells. But equally, they were waving at Claire. She waved back, loving each and every one of them.

Then as suddenly as they appeared, they had gone. The bluebells remained. Radiant still, even in the fading twilight.

"IT'S ALL OVER!" came a voice.

Ian, covered in green algae, looking like the Old Man of the Sea, was pulling himself out of the pond.

Claire couldn't help herself. Or her mouth.

"Hi Poseidon!" she called, stifling giggles, "Where's your trident?"

"IT'S ALL OVER!" he repeated, "ME AND YOU! OUR ENGAGEMENT! FINISHED! YOU DID NOTHING TO HELP!"

He lost his footing and slipped back in the water.

Claire, could no longer stifle her giggles and burst out laughing.

"Hey Mr Entrepreneur! Why don't you turn the pond into a marina?" she shouted.

"I DON'T WANT TO SET FOOT ON THIS LOUSY ISLAND EVER AGAIN!" he said, dragging himself across the grass, dripping water and weed. "EVER!"

Claire closed her eyes thankfully.

"Herm Island won't weep for you," she thought to herself as Ian cursed his way to the drive to get back to Sea Holly.

"Mind you dry off and wipe your feet before you go in," she called.

She made her way to the White House Hotel. They would find her a room, she was sure. She wondered about the fairy Ian had trod on.

She was sure he would be alright. They must have a way of looking after their own.

She was right.

When she woke up in the morning, on the bedside table, was a single crushed bluebell. And a note on which was written in a spidery hand 'All is well. Thank you.'

∾

THE HERM MIRACLE

*Imagine a group of inept thespians accompanied by
an unruly bunch of children performing the medieval
miracle play 'Noah's Flood' in Herm's St. Tugual's
Chapel, and you have the basis of the tale of 'The
Herm Miracle'. Because the narrator of this tale, Dev,
is a 'simple soul', loyal but not the sharpest member
of the troupe, I decided to write his story in words of
no more than 5 letters, just as a challenge; and they
all are, apart from the word 'miracle' itself which
appears (miraculously) right at the end of the story. I
can't help thinking that St. Tugual himself would look
down, smiling upon these shenanigans.*

I think most folk like me; tho' some look down on me.
Mike says 'when you don't worry what folk think Dev,
then you will be happy'. So, I do stop my worry. Most folk
treat me fair 'cos I do stuff for them. I'm a right smart 'gofer' I am.

One dude once said 'Yeah, I see why they call you gofer.
You look like one.'

I went on the web to find some gofer pics. There is a
'gofer' spelt odd, with a 'ph' in place of a 'f'. There be loads
of pics of the 'gofer' with the 'ph'. It's a beast from the USA.
There be a word that begin with 'indig...' means it comes
from that place only. I can't spell very well tho I'm OK with
short words, and even then, I spell some wrong.

I stare at the pics of the 'gofer' spelt with the 'ph' and
then I look in the glass. Wot I see is like wot is in those
pics, I have to own. There is buck teeth and rings round

the eyes (like my specs) and a daft look. It makes me sad. That this is how folk see me. Well, some folk.

When I tell Mike, he says 'Dev. It's what's in a man. You're a good guy Dev. And I am going to take you to Herm with me.'

Herm. I have not heard of Herm. (Herne Bay I do know; I did work on a farm in Kent with my Ma and Pa til they hev no more use for me and sent me on my way).

Mike is a man of the stage; he put on plays. He do the Bard and farce and some sad plays too. He gets his cast of folk from all over and he work them hard. Often he gets cross and shout at them. Mike lets me work for him. I am his gofer; gofer with the 'f' that is, not the 'ph'.

I like being Mike's gofer. The stuff I does seems to make him happy. He never ever shout at me.

One day he say to me: "Dev, I don't know what I'd do if I didn't have you here."

That made me feel real good, when he said that. Real warm, in my tummy.

So, we are off to Herm to do a play in a kirk. I hev found Herm on the web; it is a tiny isle in the midst of the sea. It hev a small kirk called St. Tugal. I don't think I spelt that right, so I shall call it St. T. It is very old they say. Mike is doin' a play known as 'Noah's Flood.' It is an old play from the Mid Age. Folk who work in a type of trade used to do it on a cart. We are going to do it in St. T's Kirk. On Herm. In the midst of the sea. And I am right proud.

～

So now we are on the Isle of Herm – me, Mike and the cast of Noah's Flood. We stay in tents in a big field. Some of us do share, but me and Mike have a tent each.

I have never slept in a tent, tho' I did once sleep rough

for a night or two in some big city when my mum and dad did kick me out.

The tent is nice, and I have a big warm bag to snug up in.

At the break of day, after bread, jam and tea, we all trek up to St. T's, the kirk I told you about. It is a tiny kirk with an L-shape and it is very old and very nice – just right for Noah's Flood I'd say.

At the front of the kirk is an altar and this be our stage. It isn't too big but Mike says if we take the front two rows in each limb of the 'L-shape' out, it'll give us a bit more room. This is one of my jobs, so I set to movin' the seats into a room in the small house next door.

There be nine cast in all – Noah, Mrs Noah, their three sons and the sons' wives.

That's eight. Oh yes, God is also in it – at the start and at the end.

Now you'll be sayin' to each other – what about the live-stock? I was comin' to that.

～

Ten mins to the start of the show, and no Noah. I am to run down to the pub and see if he is there, for he do have a love of the ale. Just as I set off, he turn up and he is very drunk. They sit him in the open air and we give him water and latte. I am told to get the kids in order. You asked about the live-stock. Well that's where the kids come in.

Now I have seen to cows and sheep but never kids and they look scary to me. They make so much noise. The lion do poke the tiger with a stick, the sheep do bleat, to try to get it right, I think, but it do sound rank. Then the horse ask to go to the WC but (1) I do not know if it is a boy or a girl and (2) I think the WC is way down the hill by the pub and (3) I do not think there is time.

A good lady come out of her house and allow the child to use her WC, so that is OK. The rhino is now tryin' to stab all the rest with his horn, but it is only made of card and I worry that he might break it. The hippo, a surly girl in a grey suit too tight for her, has sat down and will not get up, even when she is told she can have an ice cream. She just will not move.

The hyena do laugh at all of us and the bleat of the sheep do grate on me. I have never had a need to slap a body before, but I would love to slap that sheep.

Then the ape say she got fleas in her ape-suit and she start to rub her back agin the wall, when great bits of her fur do start to fall off.

"Hey, stop that," I say, but she make a very rude sign at me, picks up her fur and start to shove it down the top of the suit of the hippo, who then do start to scream, folds her arms and still won't get up.

Then I do smell a funny smell in the air.

"What's that?" I shout.

It is the skunk, which I s'pose is right for him if he do act the part, but what he must have had for lunch, I do not care to guess.

In the kirk, Noah's three sons are at the back; they do play a game of poker. Mike does not think this is right, bein' a kirk and all.

"Go and stop them Dev," he say. I go in and stand over them.

"It's the gofer," Ham say to me, "What's up gofer? Want some nuts?"

I tell them to stop the poker game. They laugh. I tell them again. Ham say to me:

"You ain't half ugly gofer."

I say "If you didn't have to act in a play in a bit, I'd black your eye. Then I'd bash your nose."

I did learn to stand up for my own self, 'cos no one would do it for me. I do now. And right proud of me I am too for doing it.

I fix Ham with my glare and he fix me with his, and you know, folks, he give up and says to the other two sons of Noah:

"Game's over guys; stack 'em." Then he look at me and say, "I'll deal with you later."

By now, Mrs Noah is in a panic over her skirt, which will not stay up.

"Fix it Dev," Mike says to me.

Now Mrs Noah is known as a bit of a lady's lady who don't like men to touch her, so I see the look of fear on her face as I move near her with a large pin. I don't know if it was the pin she was afrit of or me, bein' a male and all. Never mind, I got round the back of her and let the pin do its work. She do not like me at her rear end and there are a few tears and a small cry at one point when I do miss the dress with the pin and get her rump in its place. She is not a happy bunny on which I pin her tail.

Shem's wife do bawl out. She is on her phone.

"The rat!" she cries out, "He's two timed me. That's it. I can't go on. I'm too upset."

Mike stare at her as if she has lost her mind.

"Dev!" he call out to me, "Talk to her."

Shem's wife's face is red, her eyes full of tears and she look at me as if she will lose it any time. I do not like to talk to this lady. She do scare me. I think if I say the wrong thing, she will claw my eyes out. She is like that.

But no. She don't go for me. She start tryin' to claw Ham's wife's eyes out in place of mine.

"You snide cow!" she say. "You bin havin' it off with my man."

It's vexin' bein' in show biz. I stand and wait for the storm to blow over. I'm sure the folks who watch our play won't see the claw marks down Ham's wife's face and Shem's wife's puffy eyes and runny nose. As long as she don't check her phone on stage. Mike would not like that.

The kirk do fill up with folk and there are a lot of them. They stand at the back and sit in the aisle. It is what we call in show biz a full house.

I check the kids. There do not seem to be any probs there. The tiger has got the stick off the lion so there be no more pokin'. Well, not much. The sheep and the hyena are quiet now – for those that are not, I have tape ready – tape that I can stick over a mouth.

The ape has no fur left on her back at all, so she has to make sure she do face the front all the time. And the skunk still do not smell at all nice but only the front row will know.

The sons are ready to go on, Mr Noah is a bit more sober and is goin' over his lines.

Every so often he do aid his mind with the help of a small flask he keep hid in his robe.

Mike give me the thumb up sign. Show time, he do mime to me.

I press a knob on my key board to start the sound. St T's do fill up with the sound of Duran Duran with 'Girls on Film.' I stop the sound and see Mike with his head in his hands. This time I press the knob, the right sound come out.

'Tis a piece of holy music that sound like the sea. And the play is ready to begin…

Only it don't.

I see Mike mime at me:

"Where is God?"

Now I know that this is a big query that a lot of folk ask and I think why do Mike ask me this now, with 'Noah's Flood' about to start.

All is not well. He mouth at me again "Where the hell is God, Dev?" and I know what he be sayin' now. God opens the show – I mean the man who play the part of God, and he is not here.

God has to come on at the start and say a bit and then call Noah and tell him to build the Ark.

There is real worry in Mike's face. God is not here.

The crew do go out and scout round for God, and I think upon this.

Here we are in St. T's kirk and there is no God. It do not make sense.

Mike come over to me, near to tears. I do not like to see Mike upset, so I say:

"Mike. Fear not. I will be God."

He look at me as if I am crazy, but I go ahead. I put on a spare robe that hangs on the back of a chair, take my specs off and ruff up my hair.

I am about to walk out to start the show and I see Shem's wife is on her phone again, so I grab it from her and put it in the folds of my robe. She looks cross but does not speak.

Then, tryin' to look like God, I walk out in front of the crowd. Mike do start the music again.

Now you might find it hard to take, but I have seen that play done so many times that I do know all the words. I could never read it mind, on the page, but I know it all – in my head.

So I, Dev, go out there, and play God. My voice do swell

and fill that tiny kirk, as I spout God's lines.

I have never acted in my life afore, but I do give it my all now. I just reach the bit where I call upon Mr Noah to build his ark, when Shem's wife's phone do go off in my robe.

The crowd are quiet. They wait.

I whip the phone out, press it to stop it, put it to my ear and I say:

"Hello? Yes, I will see Mr Noah now. Send him up."

And the folk do laugh and clap. And I see Mike grin at the side of the kirk, so I know I done right.

Mr Noah come in and his nose do not look all that red from his time in the pub. I say to him to build the ark; how big it should be and then I exit. And the crowd clap again as I go off, and I feel right proud.

The play go with no hitch at all. Well, not many. The skunk smell so bad we do not let him go on. Mr Noah do lose his lines at one point but a quick swig from his flask gets him going again.

Mrs Noah's pin do come out and she all but lose her skirt. She do hev to hold it up with both hands and when she make to wave her arms, she gets near to losin' it agin. Then Shem's wife hev a go at Ham's wife.

"Cow!" she do shout, "Cow!"

At which point, the child who do play the cow think she has to come on. She walk on to the stage.

"Moo!" she say.

Shem goes on to get the child, sayin', "Sorry, the cow's got loose."

Then comes the bit where all the wild life hev to come in two by two. Only it don't. It comes in dribs and drabs. The ape do stop to pick up bits of fur which do drop off her still. The zebra, whose eye-holes in her mask are too small, do fall over the ape. The hippo do turn round and kick the lion who is now pokin' her with his stick.

The folk laugh and clap.

It is near the end of the play. It is God's turn again, so I get ready to go on. He has to make the sun shine at the end of the play to show Noah he has done good.

"Thou shalt have no other gods afore me!"

I turn. It is God who stand by me – the real God, the man who was to do the part.

"How dare you take my place?" he say.

"You were not here," I say to him.

"I went into the wild," God said, his eyes on fire. "There are times when I need to be alone."

"Not when you are in a play," I say. "I had to take your place. The show must go on."

"I will go on now," God say.

"You can't. What will folk think? A new God they don't know. I'm God now."

"I AM GOD!" God say, "And I will play my part."

He do scare me, God do. But I stand by what I say.

On the stage the live-stock bleat, roar, neigh, moo and bark. There is a pong in the air. Even the skunk has got back in the act. Only one God has to go on now. And I think it must be me. I make to go on. God holds me back. He tries to go on. I hold him back.

Then this girl come from out the blue. She go up to the other God and say:

"Dad, let Dev be God. 'Tis only right. You went off into the wild. And he's good."

I look at this girl and some odd sense come over me. She is right nice to look at.

God turns to me.

"You are a good God?" he ask.

"I am a very good God," I reply.

"Then go out and cast thy word, good God."

The girl smile at me and wink. My heart kind of turns over.

By now, the noise of the live-stock is very loud. The pong is rife an' all.

"Dev!" I see Mike wavin' fit to bust. "Be God!"

I walk out. And the live-stock do cease their noise. All eyes are on me. The folk who watch are still and quiet. It is my time.

I say my lines about how Mr Noah done good and do you know what? As I reach the end, the kirk light up. The Herm sun do come out from the cloud and the whole kirk is warm and sunny. The folk look round them and up at the stain glass. One of them is a man in a boat, and that one is very vivid. None other than Noah. And his ark.

The play end. I go off about to cry. It all went wrong. I hev let Mike down. I stand there, tears comin' out of my shut eyes. Then Mike comes up and puts his arm round me.

'Hear that Dev?'

I hear the crowd clap. They do clap and cheer. Loud. Very loud.

"Take a bow Dev," Mike say, "You made the show."

I go on and the crowd clap even more. The girl smile at me and that is great. The real God seems happy. The cast clap me. Even Ham who was going to sort me out later.

After the show, the girl come up to me.

"I'm Abbi," she say, "And you were great Dev."

And she kiss me. I think we like each other and will see each other again. I give her a hug. I see God spyin' on us. And I think…what will it be like to have God as a dad-in-law?

I do learn a new word that day.

MIRACLE!

It have more than five letters. The play was a MIRACLE play. And it was a MIRACLE. The sun shone at the end of the play and that was a MIRACLE. To meet Abbi was a MIRACLE. To be able to love her is a MIRACLE. If she love me, that will be a MIRACLE an' all.

See, they do occur.

And to have been part of one, makes me feel right proud.

∼

DANCING FOR PIERRE

Here is a tale that ended up differently to what was intended. When first conceived, it was to be a humorous story about a simple girl gulled into believing that dancing around the stone obelisk on the sand dunes of Herm (adjacent to the Common at the North end) would result in her getting a boyfriend. It became a much more serious, emotional story charting the 'friendship' between two women from childhood to adulthood and how their fates are tied up with that same obelisk, Pierre-Aux-Rats. This is one of my favourites although I have no idea where it came from. Equally, Pierre-Aux-Rats stands as one of my favourite locations on Herm.

Georgie read the email and felt the blood draining from her face. Her skin was clammy; her heart went into overdrive.

She read it again, in disbelief.

Kim? An email from Kim Goodison? She read it a third time.

"Hi Georgie, I know it's been a long time, but can we meet? Please? Pretty please? The usual place on Herm? Our special place? You can't say no. Your true and loving friend, Kim."

Georgie, her mind befuddled and numb, didn't hear Kirk come into the room. He touched her shoulder gently and she jumped a mile.

"What's up with you?" he said, "You act like you've seen a ghost."

"I have," Georgie said. "A ghost from my past. I've had an email. If you can guess who from, I'll treat you to a slap-up meal."

"Your late lamented Auntie Gladys," Kirk joked.

"Kim Goodison." The name almost stuck in her throat. He stared at her, open-mouthed.

"Yes." She nodded, "That knocked you back, didn't it?"

"What the hell does that weird wacky old Goth want? After all these years."

"Thirteen to be precise." Georgie had counted them since their last fateful meeting, each and every one. "I dread to think."

"Well? Are you going?"

"Of course not."

"You don't sound very certain."

Georgie wasn't. She wasn't very certain at all.

She shrugged it off.

"You guessed wrong, so you can treat me tonight. I need to partake of some fruit of the vine."

She couldn't stop thinking about that email. Why on earth did Kim want her to rush back to Herm?

The usual place.

Pierre-Aux-Rats, a strange granite obelisk that stood high on the sand dunes at the bleak North End of the island, overlooking the vast expanse of common.

Their special place.

~

They were year 7 schoolgirls camping on Herm – an adventure holiday – giggling in tents late at night, squirming around in thick pyjamas in sleeping bags. Orienteering during the day. Swimming at Belvoir Bay if it was warm enough.

They had taken the cliff path to Shell Beach, a litter of schoolchildren chattering their way around the headland. When they reached the common, Kim stopped and drew in her breath.

"What's that?" she gasped.

Georgie followed her gaze and saw it too. The stone obelisk.

"That's Pierre-Aux-Rats," Miss Probin, their teacher, told them. "Built by the stone quarrymen. The first one got pulled down, so they re-built it."

"It looks like a finger pointing at the sky," Georgie said.

Kim was still staring.

"It's a Pyrrhic symbol," she breathed, "That's what it is, a Pyrrhic symbol."

"What's one of those?" Georgie asked. Much later they learnt Kim had got the wrong word.

"A sign of fertility," she told Georgie in confidence, and Kim knew all about these things. She had knowledge far beyond her years. "If you touch that and dance round it, you'll get a good husband, a happy marriage, a great sex life and loads and loads of babies."

"I'm not sure I…" Georgie began.

"Not now, stupid," Kim broke in, "I mean when we're grown-ups."

Georgie couldn't think that far ahead, and said nothing; it was unwise to contradict Kim.

That night, in their sleeping bags, they messed about as usual…shining torches in their mouths pretending to be zombies, tickling each other, telling ghost stories, being rude about their teachers …all very innocent but it had an edge because it was forbidden. They should have been fast asleep.

Georgie was always the one with the conscience.

"Kim, I think we should sleep now," she said, "Got to be up early."

Kim turned on her with a ferocity Georgie found frightening.

"Why do you always have to spoil things?" she snapped, "You can be so boring Georgie, do you know that? Boring!"

And she flounced over in her sleeping bag.

Georgie hadn't meant to upset her. Kim was her friend. She lay there miserably, staring at Kim's rigid back.

"Kim…" she said, putting out a hand to touch her.

Kim shrugged it away.

Georgie flicked her torch off, to settle for the night. But Kim wasn't finished. She shone her torch in Georgie's eyes.

"Your trouble is Georgie, you don't know how to treat your friends," she said, "You…abuse friendship. What have you got to say for yourself?"

"I'm sorry Kim," Georgie mumbled, "I won't upset you again."

"That's better," Kim said. "Because if you do, you know what'll happen, don't you?"

"No, what?" Georgie didn't really want to know. She just wanted to keep Kim on her side.

"The spirits of the common will get you. Miss Probin told me about them. They get inside you and make you barren."

"What's that mean?" Georgie asked.

"Don't you know anything?" Kim said. "It means you won't be able to have babies when you grow up. Don't you want to have babies?"

"I hadn't really thought…"

"Of course you do. That's why we must dance on the Common around Pierre-Aux-Rats. Around the Pyrrhic Symbol."

"I don't know…"

"And we have to dance…NAKED!"

Georgie uttered a horrified gasp and pulled her sleeping bag tightly around her.

"Kim. That would be…WRONG!"

"There you go again. There's no hope for you. You spoil everything."

Kim turned her back, adopting a defensive foetal position and didn't speak again that night.

Georgie's face was wet with tears. What could she do to win the friendship of this girl she so much looked up to?

There were certain things she wouldn't do; what Kim had just suggested was one of them. It tore Georgie apart. She cried about it for days. Until Kim came up to her at school a couple of weeks later, took her hand and said:

"I want us to be friends again."

～

Georgie packed her suitcase methodically. Kirk stood in the bedroom doorway, watching.

"I won't be long," she told him, "You've got a few days off. We don't have to leave the kids with anybody. There's plenty of food in. You could take them out for a MacDonald's. Only once mind."

Kirk said nothing.

"Well don't just stand there. At least tell me I'm crazy."

"I think you are," he said, "I think you're as crazy as she is."

"Kirk, we've been friends since we were eleven. I have to go. She might need my help."

"I'd like to think you're going out of curiosity, Georgie, not because you feel you owe her. For God's sake, you told me she bit you once!"

~

They were in year 9. Georgie thought Kim looked beautiful, slim, dark with eyes like bottomless pools. Beside her, Georgie felt frumpish and ungainly.

Kim stopped her in the corridor one day, looking flushed and excited.

"Georgie. There's something we have to do."

"What is it?"

"You'll see."

Kim took her hand. Georgie followed without question. If it was something Kim wanted to do, it must be important. They stopped outside the pottery studio.

"It's a secret," Kim said, "No telling. Promise?" Kim put her finger on her lips. Georgie did the same.

"I promise."

The pottery studio was empty. On the bench at the back of the room, a piece of polythene sheet was hiding something.

"Look!" proclaimed Kim dramatically, pulling the sheet away.

Georgie stared. Kim laughed.

"What is it?" Georgie said.

"Don't you recognise it?" Kim said, "It's Pierre-Aux-Rats."

It was indeed a clay representation of the obelisk on the sand-dunes of Herm. The wet clay glistened. Kim had obviously only just made it.

"Hug me!" she said.

"What?"

"Give me a hug, stupid. Please? Pretty please?"

She stood there, arms outstretched, waiting for Georgie, who came forward into Kim's arms. She felt them tighten around her, felt Kim's mouth on the side of her face, then screamed in pain. She staggered back, her hand to her ear.

"You bit my ear!" Georgie said, "Kim. You bit me."

Taking her hand away from her ear, Georgie saw blood on her fingers.

"Quick now," Kim said, apparently ignorant of the injury she had inflicted. She took Georgie's hand and wiped her fingers against the clay effigy, leaving a smear of Georgie's blood there. She offered Georgie a clay cutting knife.

"Cut my thumb," she said, "Then our blood will mingle together on Pierre."

"No Kim" Georgie said, "I can't do that."

A look of contempt crossed Kim's face.

"I knew you'd let me down. Again," she said, "Just like you wouldn't dance with me on the common. Oh well, I'll just have to do it myself."

Kim sliced her thumb with the knife. Georgie watched in horror as she rubbed her thumb against the clay statuette.

"Kim, I think you need to get that seen to," Georgie said, staring in concern at Kim's thumb which was bleeding copiously, "I need to get you to Sick Bay. You might need stitches."

Kim was smiling. Blood was pouring from her thumb but she was smiling.

"We are blood-sisters in the sight of Pierre-Aux-Rats. Now, some of our hair." Deftly and before Georgie realised what was happening, Kim sliced a lock of Georgie's hair off, followed by her own. She intertwined them and worked them into the clay together with their blood.

Kim scooped up the model and popped it into a Tesco carrier-bag as a teacher came into the room.

"How does it feel, blood-sister?" Kim whispered,

"Aren't you proud? Our fates are bound together in this clay model. We must return to Pierre-Aux-Rats. A pilgrimage. To pay homage to Pierre. What do you say?"

There was nothing Georgie could say.

But yes, she did feel a strange sense of pride. Blood-sisters in the sight of Pierre-Aux-Rats.

～

It had been an awkward goodbye at the airport. Her children, six-year-old Hannah and four-year-old Hamish, clung to her, not wanting her to go. Kirk made it plain he wasn't over the moon either, but said nothing. Georgie thought that was worse. A dull ache gripped her stomach when she looked back at them standing by the car. Darling Kirk, the fantastic man in her life and her two adorable children. A strong urge was talking to her:

"Go back! Don't be stupid Georgie! Why are you leaving your wonderful family? For her? For Kim? Look what you are leaving behind. Just look over your shoulder. Look at Hannah, wiping her tears away with one hand and waving pathetically with the other. And Hamish doesn't understand what's happening. Look at his little face! LOOK, Georgie! Go back."

Georgie didn't go back. A stronger voice pulled her forward.

Please? Pretty please? You can't say no.

We are blood-sisters in the sight of Pierre-Aux-Rats.

Besides, she had sworn an oath.

～

It was Kim's idea. An Easter revision session on Herm Island, before A-levels. A cottage, Kim said, self-catering.

"We'll live on fast-food and intellect." She laughed in that careless way of hers.

There was a strange passion in her laugh. Georgie

could almost see a vision of the obelisk reflected in Kim's eyes. It was time for their pilgrimage – to pay homage to Pierre. Kim had grown ever more beautiful – dark-haired Kim with the come-hither eyes.

The boys queued up to have their hearts broken. Beside her, Georgie wasn't exactly fat, but compared to Kim, she was. Boys didn't queue up after *her*. They approached her in the school library to ask how to solve some chemistry problem – calculating electrode potentials or a redox titration. Boys wanted Georgie for her brain. They wanted Kim for a different reason entirely.

Did she envy Kim? In a way, she did, but not bitterly. Kim was her friend and deep down, Georgie loved her, even though Kim didn't really love her back.

So, at the age of 18, at Easter, before their A-levels, the blood-sisters returned to Herm.

They sat in the cottage drinking cider. Little revision had been done, mainly because of Kim's incessant chattering. Georgie's revision book was open at a page entitled 'Transition Metal Complexes'.

"That looks boring," sneered Kim.

"It's OK," said Georgie.

"Is thallium a transition metal?"

"No," Georgie said, surprised that Kim had even heard of thallium.

"I've decided my birthstone is thallium." Kim giggled. "I no longer have a Pyrrhic symbol. I now have a thallic symbol."

She burst out laughing. Georgie managed a smile.

"Do you remember what I said we should do?" Kim asked, "Back then? Our adventure holiday? When we were eleven?"

"No," Georgie said, knowing full well what Kim was

talking about, but not wanting to encourage her.

"You do," Kim said, mischievous fire flashing in her eyes. "I can understand why you didn't want to take your clothes off and dance. Because you were…bulky at the time."

Bulky! That word hurt Georgie even more than if Kim had called her fat.

"You've lost a lot of weight," Kim carried on regardless, "You don't look so puffy and abnormal as you used to. But let's face it, Georgie, you're still quite big, aren't you? So, I've brought us something to dance in."

She flitted into the bedroom; Georgie heard her rummaging in her suitcase. She ran her hand across her face and was surprised to find that the back of her hand was wet. She hadn't even realised she was crying.

Kim emerged triumphant holding up two long grey garments.

"Ta-dah!" she sang, "Pagan robes."

"What?" Georgie said.

"I've researched it," Kim said, excited. "There was a lot of paganism on Herm. But there was this monk. Saint Magloire. He punished the pagans for their practices. But we don't care about him, do we?"

"Why should we?"

"Because tonight, Georgie-baby, we are going to dance for Pierre. On the common. We are blood-sisters in his sight, aren't we? Well, aren't we?"

With a flourish, she produced the clay effigy of the obelisk they had given their blood and hair to, when they were fourteen. She placed it on the table and offered her hand, which Georgie reluctantly took.

"Put your other hand on Pierre," Kim said.

Georgie placed a tentative finger on the side of the clay

statue. Kim did the same.

"Now! Say the oath."

Georgie didn't like the way this was going at all. "What oath?" she said.

"The oath of allegiance. Alright. I'll say it and you just say 'I swear' or something at the end. OK?"

"I suppose," Georgie said.

Kim closed her eyes, raised her head and chanted:

"We, blood-sisters in the sight of Pierre-Aux-Rats do solemnly swear that we shall remain as such, forever. Should one ever have need of the other, then the blood-sisters shall come together without question."

Kim stood there, eyes closed, head up for a moment longer and then said:

"Go on. Say 'I swear!'"

Georgie whispered the words without any real conviction.

"Right," Kim said derisively, "Same old disappointing Georgie."

"I said it, didn't I?" Georgie protested.

"You could have said it as if you meant it. Still, you now have the chance to prove yourself."

The old animosity had taken charge of Kim's face.

"How?" asked Georgie.

"Put your coat on and grab your robe," Kim said, "We're going dancing!"

There was a keen wind cutting through them as they crossed the common by torchlight.

"We have to touch Pierre first," Kim said, "Then we'll come back to the stone circle. That's where we dance."

As they pushed their way through the scrub, Kim swore.

"What's wrong?" Georgie asked her.

"I've torn my bloody tights on the brambles."

Georgie had to stifle a laugh. Here they were, about to enact a weird ritual in a stone circle near a strange monolith at midnight and Kim was concerned about her tights. Georgie didn't dare laugh out loud though.

Kim's face was a few inches from hers as they stood there with their hands against Pierre-Aux-Rats. The granite felt cold to Georgie's touch but Kim's breath was warm.

"Hi blood-sister," Kim said.

"Hi blood-sister," Georgie said back.

Above them, towered Pierre. Night after night, he eternally pointed his finger at the stars or the clouds or whatever regaled the sky that particular night. For ever and always.

"Time to get into our robes," Kim said, "Let's dance."

And they did. In and out of the remains of the Neolithic tombstones they danced, skipped, two-stepped, jived, span, twirled, bopped, bumped and grinded, shimmied, shuffled, sometimes together, sometimes apart. Kim whooped. Georgie, her blood rushing and her mood ecstatic, echoed the whoop. Then they yelled out together. Faster they danced, faster still, getting more manic by the minute, two eighteen-year olds dressed like pagan priests.

Georgie suddenly realised for the first time in her life, she was enjoying an experience. With Kim.

Until she caught sight of Kim slipping out of her robe and dancing in her underwear.

"KIM!" she shrieked, "DON'T! You'll get pneumonia!"

Before Kim could undress any further, she fell to the ground with a scream and lay still.

Georgie knelt over her.

"Kim, what's wrong?"

Kim's face was white with fear. She was shivering uncontrollably.

"I saw him, Georgie!" she whispered through her chattering teeth.

"Saw who Kim?"

"Saint Magloire. The monk who despises pagans. He was standing on the sand-dunes. Watching us. He's going to punish me Georgie. Help me. Remember the oath."

Georgie didn't get any sleep that night. She lay awake with Kim shivering in her arms. Kim's eyes were wide and scared, her face pallid and she was freezing cold.

At one point, she became very agitated.

"Somebody's knocking at the door, Georgie. Can't you hear it?"

Georgie said she couldn't.

"It's Saint Magloire. He's come to punish me. Go to the door Georgie. Tell him I'm sorry. No, tell him I'm not here. Please?"

Georgie opened the door. There was no-one. A bright moon hung in the sky, but the wind was still active and cold. Georgie returned to Kim.

"Did you send him away?" Kim asked, "Please say you did Georgie."

"Yes. I told him you weren't here," Georgie said gently. "He's gone away."

"I love you Georgie," Kim said and fell into an uneasy sleep.

Georgie held her in her arms until dawn. She felt so proud. Kim, her blood-sister, had told her she loved her.

～

Georgie felt desolate on the flight. Everything she loved she had left behind. She knew it wouldn't be for long, but she'd never been away from Kirk, Hannah and Hamish before. How she missed them already. Hopefully unseen by anybody, she shed tears into her complimentary coffee. What was she getting into?

After leaving school, she didn't see Kim for another two years. She cast her mind back to that last disastrous meeting, thirteen years ago on Herm. The significance of thirteen years wasn't lost on her.

Georgie got A* grades in all her A-levels and went on to study Dentistry at Queen Mary's College. While she was there, she met Kirk Williams, who was reading Chemical Engineering. They fell in love.

Kim achieved very poor A-level results, managing to scrape entry into the University of Kent to pursue a Media Studies degree.

They kept in touch by email.

Then came Kim's suggestion of a reunion weekend on Herm, staying at the White House Hotel. Georgie was curious to see how Kim had turned out.

Georgie wasn't actually that surprised to be confronted by the 'weird wacky Goth' as Kirk had later called her, although they had never actually met. But Georgie had told Kirk a lot about her.

They sat opposite each other at dinner in the Conservatory Restaurant in the Hotel. Georgie was dressed smartly but Kim looked out of place with her punky hairstyle, piercings and visible tattoos. She wore a long black dress with a plunging neckline.

"Before you ask me about Uni…I got kicked out last year." Kim looked defiant.

"Kim, I'm so sorry."

"I didn't ask for your sympathy." It was almost a growl. "I expect you're doing brilliantly. You'll be a doctor soon."

"Dentist," Georgie corrected her gently.

"You've lost weight," Kim observed, "I preferred you fat. You look scrawny."

Kim was playing with the salt cellar. Suddenly, she pushed it over. Some salt spilt on the tablecloth.

"There, that's more bad luck." She looked up at Georgie, from her over-made-up black eyes, a slight smile on her lips. Georgie felt she was treading on glass.

"Got a love life?" Kim asked.

"I've met someone," Georgie replied, "His name's Kirk. We're in love. We'll probably get married after I qualify."

"IT'S NOT FAIR!"

As Kim shouted it, she slammed her hands on the table. Glasses trembled and clinked. Georgie glanced around embarrassed.

"Calm down, Kim, people are looking at you."

"I don't give a…" Kim stopped short, picked up a full glass of red wine and necked it in one. She glared at Georgie, her eyes not quite focussing. "I'm the one boys loved. I was the one who told you about the power of Pierre-Aux-Rats. I was the one who was prepared to dance starkers. I cut myself. You were the wuss who never did ANYTHING!"

"Kim. Keep your voice down."

"DON'T TELL ME WHAT TO DO, GEORGIE!"

The restaurant had gone silent. Georgie could see the Manager making his way towards them.

Kim was asked politely to leave. Georgie was not, but she followed Kim out anyway.

They stood outside the Hotel entrance. Kim's nostrils were flaring. Her make-up was smudged. Georgie wondered where the girl she had once known had gone.

"Don't look at me like that Georgie!" Kim said, her

eyes smouldering dangerously. "Don't judge me. You've no right."

"I'm not…"

"YOU ARE!"

It had started to rain and it was coming down quite hard.

"We need to get to the common," Kim said, calming a little, "To Pierre. You owe me that, at least."

"It's raining Kim. I'm already soaked through."

Kim inclined her head slightly up to Georgie. She didn't have to say 'Please? Pretty Please?' Every inch of her was screaming it silently.

Pierre-Aux-Rats it was.

They arrived at the obelisk looking like drowned rats. Kim was clutching the Tesco carrier-bag to herself. They stood in the rain, facing each other, water coursing down their faces.

"Tell me about Kirk Georgie," Kim said, taking the effigy of Pierre from the bag. "Is he handsome?"

"I think so."

"Is he virile? Is he manly? I need a virile man, Georgie. Will you lend him to me? I want a baby Georgie. You know how much I've always wanted babies. Just one will do. Will you Georgie? Please?"

"DON'T SAY PRETTY PLEASE!" Georgie screamed, "I couldn't bear it." She took a breath. "Don't you realise what you're asking is wrong, Kim?"

"The oath, Georgie! Don't forget the oath!"

"I don't CARE about the oath, Kim!"

Kim thrust the effigy towards Georgie.

"Blood-sisters Georgie. In the sight of Pierre. Our fates are entwined in this. You have to do what I ask!"

The rain had caused havoc with Kim's mascara. She

looked like an obscene twisted clown.

Again, she thrust the clay figure at Georgie.

"Let me meet Kirk. I'm sure he'll like me!"

Something welled up inside Georgie; a rage! She couldn't take any more. She grabbed the effigy of Pierre-Aux-Rats from Kim's hands, held it aloft and dashed it against the real obelisk. It broke into pieces and dropped to the ground, the rain forming clay puddles around their feet. Strands of blonde and dark hair floated on the puddles, coming apart with the movement of the water.

"THAT'S what I think of your oath, Kim!"

"You BITCH!" Kim went for Georgie's eyes with her nails. "HOW COULD YOU GEORGIE?"

Four years ago, they danced. Now, they fought.

Georgie had superior strength and threw Kim off. She collapsed at the base of her beloved Pierre-Aux-Rats, looking up at Georgie like a caged wild animal.

"Just one night," she snarled, "That's all I wanted."

"KIM! I HAVE NO INTENTION OF LETTING YOU ANYWHERE NEAR HIM!"

Georgie walked away, her tears of anger and grief mingling with the rain running down her face. Kim had never cried for *her*. Never! Georgie glanced back. She wasn't even crying now.

Georgie made a vow. This is the last time I will ever cry for you, Kim Goodison, so help me! That is my new oath!

~

Thirteen years had not wiped the bad memory of that day in the rain. But it had dulled it.

Today there was no rain. Just brilliant sunshine giving Herm warmth.

The familiar granite obelisk 'Pierre-Aux-Rats' came

into sight as Georgie turned onto the common.

As she walked towards the sand-dunes, she wasn't sure what to expect or how Kim would have turned out after thirteen years. She had not bargained for what she was about to find.

A thin wasted desultory figure sat on the base of the obelisk, head in hands. Was she crying? No, impossible. Georgie had never known Kim to cry in her life. Kim was not crying exactly, more… whimpering. Like a dog that has been accidentally shut out of a house and wants to get back in.

"Kim?" Georgie said hesitantly.

There was a pause into which you could have inserted an earthquake. Kim slowly took her hands from her eyes.

If Georgie was shocked at finding Kim in tears, it was nothing to the shock that resounded through her when she saw Kim's face.

It was tear-stained and the tears had carried her inexpertly applied make-up to just about all areas of her face. Her hair was greying beyond her age. And there was despair and tragedy etched into lines on her face. But her woe-begone expression, the misery was what shocked Georgie the most. This was not the Kim she knew. This was once a strutting chanticleer who had been knocked off her lofty perch. It horrified Georgie.

"Kim!"

What else to say? What's happened to you? Have you been ill? You look dreadful? Nothing was appropriate.

Kim was on her feet. Hugging Georgie. Engulfing her. Transferring her hot make-up stained tears on to Georgie's face. Georgie remembered the oath she swore as she walked away thirteen years ago. This is the last time I will ever cry for you, Kim Goodison, so help me. But she wanted to cry now. For Kim. Or maybe she wanted to cry for herself.

"Everything's gone so wrong with my life Georgie," Kim sobbed. "Everything I've tried to do, everything I've touched, has turned to disaster. I'm in a mess Georgie. I got in with some bad people. Everybody I've ever cared for hates me now. You don't hate me do you Georgie? Please say you don't. If you hate me, I can't go on living."

"Of course I don't hate you Kim. We're friends. Blood-sisters in the sight of Pierre, yes?"

"I was horrible Georgie," Kim went on, "I said and did horrible things to you. I need your forgiveness."

"There's nothing to forgive," Georgie assured her.

"There is, there IS," Kim insisted, "I'm not surprised you smashed that stupid clay model. I asked for too much. I realise now."

Kim broke from the embrace, but held Georgie at arm's length, looking at her with her sad, tired, ravaged eyes. Georgie couldn't help thinking that Kim looked like a little old lady, frail and fragile.

"I want you to say you forgive me."

"Kim…"

"SAY IT!"

"Alright. I forgive you Kim."

"I love you Georgie."

"I love you too, Kim."

"That's why I wanted you to come back. For me to say sorry, to have your forgiveness and to hear you say you loved me. I know it was asking a lot to bring you all this way for that, but I had to see your face as you said it."

"I do need to get back," Georgie said, "I can get the last boat to St. Peter Port and a flight tomorrow morning."

"To see your husband. And your children?"

"Yes."

Another wave of despair took Kim's face over. "I wanted babies. You know I wanted babies. I can't have them, Georgie. The doctor has told me. I'm…barren. The spirits on the common must have got me. Either them…or it's Saint Magloire's punishment. Can I come and see your babies, Georgie? Sometime?"

Georgie, who was already through the bramble pathway, stopped.

"That's probably not a good idea Kim."

"I understand," Kim said. "I'm going to dance for Pierre now. Will you join me?"

"I think I've outgrown that Kim. I'm sorry."

Georgie walked back across the common. On impulse, she stopped and turned.

The pathetic figure was dancing in the stone circle. Kim danced slowly but with great expression. She reminded Georgie of a picture of a sylph she had once seen. Kim was singing as well; Georgie could just hear her. She didn't know the song, but it seemed to fit the dance. The combination of song and dance was soulful. And in that moment, Kim became beautiful again.

Georgie stood and watched for a few minutes.

Then she slowly retraced her steps.

Back towards her blood-sister.

∼

LATE NIGHT IN MONK'S BAR

The Monk's Bar in the White House Hotel is notoriously haunted by the ghost of a monk, hence its name. This has to be a setting for a story, even if only to unnerve those staff who have the misfortune to work the late shift and clear up, long after the last guest has staggered off to bed. But it had to have an angle, so I thought what about somebody who comes to work on Herm, who has ghosts of her own to exorcise and actually volunteers for as many late shifts as she can get? She is the only protagonist in these tales to be portrayed as an employee of the island, but she is entirely fictional. Meet Lara Manning, a very troubled young lady...

Lara Manning's obsession with ghosts and all things supernatural started long before she came to Herm.

It began when she baby-sat for the Gibsons – in that big house on the other side of the street, that rambling mansion of a place, that dust emporium; what was a young family like the Gibsons doing in a place like that anyway?

Amy Gibson was a sweet five-year old. Lara would play games with her, tell her a story and put her to bed. She was a perfect child to baby-sit for. No fuss, straight to bed, straight to sleep.

Then Lara would get her books out and study for her A-levels in Maths, History, Sociology and Psychology. Whilst getting paid for it.

Life was perfect. Until the night she found out that the dust emporium, rambling and expansive, with places that

Lara dared not go, was haunted.

First the wailings from the empty rooms. Then the unexplained banging on the ceiling.

The ephemeral veil-like mist that hung about the hall, with an agenda of its own.

The red-glowing eyes at the far, dark end of the house.

Lara continued to baby-sit, but she dreaded Amy's bedtime, because that's when it started.

Studying became difficult. Lara, once an open-faced happy girl, became ferrety, edgy, with eyes that darted in all directions at a rate of knots. Looking for 'ghosts'.

Everybody noticed the change – parents, school-friends, teachers. The Gibsons began to question her suitability for baby-sitting. Even Amy noticed the change. The bed-time story wasn't as exciting, the games not as much fun.

And why did Lara keep looking out of the door, shining her torch down the corridor?

Lara now spent the whole evening in Amy's bedroom. It was tranquil there, as if the evil spirits were barred. Whilst Amy slept, Lara crept into her room, sat in the corner with her torch to study.

The banging and the wailings never went away though.

Lara knew it would eventually manifest itself. She was scared witless every time she was in the house, that this would be the night. Trying to psych herself up for it, she had no idea how she would respond.

Sure enough.

One night, she left the sanctuary of Amy's room to grab a coffee. Immediately, she was aware of the icy atmosphere; at the top of the stairs, she heard a low-pitched devilish hum that came from everywhere at once; glancing back towards Amy's room, she saw it at the end of the corridor.

Some sort of monk. Where its eyes should have been, glowing red luminescence. Above its head, a visible aura of evil, its arms outstretched towards her; it was chanting her name, in a low primeval voice.

"La-ra! La-ra!"

But it sounded as if there were hundreds of them.

Now it was outside Amy's door. There was no way back into Lara's sanctuary.

It was creeping towards her.

The Gibsons returned that evening to find Lara sitting in the front garden, clasping her knees, staring fixedly at the house, muttering: 'You cannot leave the house, spirit. You are bound inside the place you were generated.'

Amy was in bed, fast asleep, safe and sound. But Lara was never asked to baby-sit again.

Then came three years at University reading Psychology and in her spare time, studying Parapsychology. Needing to atone. Never to run away from the supernatural again. Trying to rationalise her fear. Trying to cope.

Three years healing. Then a gap year.

And Herm Island.

～

Lara hated the graveyard shift in the Monk's Bar. A few of the other White House Hotel bar staff did too. There were reports of a sudden cooling. An odd unexplained bump. Even the sighting of a cowled figure, hazy and for a few seconds.

The Monk's Bar was reckoned to be notoriously haunted by the ghost of a Monk, but nobody took it seriously.

By day.

But by night, on your own, you might feel a little discomfited, on edge, listening and looking for something, whatever it was – to catch sight of the monk, to hear an eerie shuffling from the bar as you cleared coffee cups in the lounge, to feel the icy coldness in the air, to smell the sudden scent of incense wafting by you or to taste the evil bitterness in the water you were drinking.

Lara Manning had greatest cause to believe that the Monk's Bar was haunted – and she, above all, hated the graveyard shift.

Nobody could understand therefore why she accepted every shift that became available, why Lara was always eager to swap shifts so she could be there. It was clear that Lara Manning wanted to be in the Monk's Bar late at night, although nobody knew why.

Lara knew. Never mind the Monk; Lara Manning was haunted by a past ghost. And it would not go away. Until she faced her own fear.

One particular night there was a storm raging outside. The Trident had been cancelled so no-one could get on or off the island. The rain lashed at the windows with unprecedented fury and the high winds screamed. It was a night for ghost stories, to be told around the fire in the lounge, amongst lots of people.

There were no people in the Monk's Bar that night. No-one except Lara.

Alone, her arms around herself in a feeble effort to keep warm, she was shivering. She didn't want to leave the sanctuary behind the bar to clear the tables. But she knew she had to. She couldn't understand why she felt so cold. The last thing she believed was that she would see the Monk. And yet…

Where the first vibrations came from, Lara wasn't sure. Her eyes caught sight of the decorative porcelain cow hanging from the centre of the ceiling; it was revolving.

A breeze surely. With all that wind outside, why shouldn't there be a breeze blowing through the bar.

Get a grip, Lara told herself. Get busy. Get out in the bar and rattle those glasses and cups.

But the cups and glasses began to rattle themselves, gently at first, but definitely vibrating on the tables. A kinetic force was at work, and it was getting stronger.

More maddening than frightening, it was doing her head in. Big time. There was a way to stop it. Clear the offending items away. Suddenly she was in the Monk's Bar. She had left her sanctuary.

From the lounge, there was a crash. Somebody had dropped a cup.

"Suzi?" she called, "Is that you?"

Suzi was the evening receptionist.

She picked up two glasses, placing them on the bar. A thought flashed into her head, disconcerting and frightening:

The Monk will walk tonight.

Was it in her head, or were the words spoken aloud? It was a girl's voice that spoke them. A little girl.

It was Amy's voice. Amy Gibson, for whom she used to baby-sit.

Impossible, don't be ridiculous Lara, how could Amy be here?

Then came an incredibly loud tearing splitting noise, echoing through the bar like thunder. And terrible laughter. Lara felt unable to move. The inside of her mouth was dry and her skin was icy. She glanced up.

The monk was gone from his box.

Over the bar was a box inside which usually stood a small mannequin of a monk, almost cartoonish. If you pulled the string under the box, he moved a little. Now he had disappeared.

Lara looked at the box again. No mistake. The little monk had gone. It was a joke.

Somebody was playing on her weakness, having a laugh at her expense.

Lara cast her mind back. Had he been there earlier? Had somebody taken him? To play a trick on her?

Why should they? But the box was definitely empty.

There were plenty of people who could have faked a little girl's voice. But she couldn't remember telling anybody about her baby-sitting terror. The Gibsons said they never wanted to see her again. Lara wasn't proud of it. She had never told anybody.

She was still trying to exorcise that old ghost.

The Monk will walk tonight.

If she carried on clearing up, taking no notice of their tricks, not giving them the satisfaction, they would tire of the game. They would all have a laugh, Lara laughing the loudest of all, not cowed by their stupid antics.

She began to feel braver.

"I know what you're up to," she shouted, her voice echoing through the ground floor of the Hotel, "I suppose you think you're clever. That rattling glasses stunt was awesome. Very smart."

In reply, the tables began to vibrate again, very slightly. No glasses rattled because she had cleared them.

She heard that horrible laugh again. Lara realised they must have rigged up a speaker.

There must be wires to it, easily traceable. You couldn't hide anything like that.

Search the lounge, Lara! As she made to leave, her eyes rested on the picture to the left of the bar; wild seas crashing against rocks, startling and dramatic.

Never so much as now.

Crouched on a rock, a hand extended, was a cloaked figure. Underneath the dark cowl, Lara could see red glimmering eyes looking directly at her.

She breathed rapidly and it caught in her throat, choking her. The choke sounded like a laugh, and then she heard somebody else laughing along with her, a repeated choking mocking laugh, half-human. Like a child imitating an animal. Amy?

She continued to stare at the picture but the figure had gone.

The Monk will walk tonight.

The box above the bar was empty. Now the monk was gone from the seascape. To the right of the picture was an oak chair. Lara's eyes were drawn towards it. She knew. He would appear here next.

She backed away from the chair. Her skin felt as if a thousand insects were crawling over her. Her breath seemed to be forming ice crystals in the air.

She stared at the chair. Was it her imagination or was there an image forming – a cowled figure sitting in the chair, its head bowed. She shook her head violently from side to side as if to clear her vision. The chair was empty.

You are seeing things Lara, she told herself. Get a grip.

Then came laughter again. It was loud and demonic laughter, and it was right next to her. There was a statue of a monk on the mantelpiece. She knew it well, because she lifted it every shift to wipe away any dust from underneath it. Its hideous face was laughing, the lips moving, and it was rocking back and forth, as if shaking with the evil laughter that was emanating from it.

This couldn't be happening.

Grab hold of it, Lara. Smash it. You can always say it

was an accident. You must stop it laughing. You must. Face your fears, Lara. That's what you've always wanted to do. Your life's aim. Confront your fears!

She took a step towards the mantelpiece her hands outstretched. Grab the wretched little devil? She would strangle the thing. Except it was gone. It was dancing inside the glass jug, also standing on the mantelpiece. She could hear the sound of its feet and hands as they beat against the glass.

She moved towards the glass but it was gone again. Now it was with the seals – in the picture on the wall with the seals. It was staring at her, laughing at her. Clapping its hands like a performing circus seal.

The Monk will walk tonight.

It was doing more than that. It was leading a merry dance around the bar and it was a show put on for her benefit. Lara had a sudden thought. It's trying to drive you mad, to drive you out of your mind. It wants you insane, Lara. It wants you to be just like itself.

Don't let it Lara. Talk to it. Face your fears.

Where was it now? It was in the glass bowl. No, it had moved to the shelf on the opposite side of the Monk's Bar. It was running backwards and forwards between the candlesticks. Every so often it would stop and look at her. It had rosy cheeks and deep blue eyes and thick blue lips, but overall, its face had a look of sheer evil. And that laugh.

There was one more place where Lara thought it would appear before it returned to its box. In the picture of the sand dunes. Her eyes were drawn to it. As yet, nothing.

Where was it?

A door slammed.

The sound had come from the garden room. Lara remembering closing that door firmly. Why should it

114

slam, unless someone had opened it again? Who? The relentless storm-driven rain beat against the windows. Who had come in from those dreadful conditions?

Who, in their right mind?

The Monk will walk tonight.

Was the Monk in his right mind?

Her eyes flickered back to the framed picture of the sand-dunes.

Nothing.

She breathed a sigh of relief, but it was short lived. Somebody was in the next room.

She could hear footsteps.

A man.

A man in a wet cape was standing in the doorway, water running off him and making puddles on the floor.

Lara had never been so pleased to see anybody in her life.

"You've come just at the right time," she said. She wanted to throw herself at the man. To hug him just to make sure he was real. In spite of his wet cape.

"I know," he said, "It's hell out there. A stroll before bed was not a good idea. What's up with you? You look as if…"

"I've seen a ghost!" Lara finished the sentence. "Did you know the Monk's Bar was haunted? By the self-same Monk it's named after. Well…I saw him tonight."

"Come on," he said. "You don't believe all that stuff, do you?"

"I wish I didn't," Lara said, "But you see…"

"Hang on," he said, "Get me a drink first. Then you can tell me."

"Of course, of course." The words came quickly, borne on Lara's rapid breathing.

"Coffee please, and a Benedictine on the side," he said.

"Certainly sir," she said, "Take a seat. I'll bring it."

He took off his wet cape placing it on one of the tables. He sat in the oak chair – where earlier, she had expected to see the ghost of the monk.

Lara busied herself. It all seemed so stupid now there was somebody here. When the drinks were ready, she carried them on a tray into the bar.

She stopped, eyes wide.

Where was he? Where was the late-night guest? The oak chair was empty. He was gone. So was his cape. So were the puddles of water on the floor that had poured off him when he came in. Water doesn't dry that quickly. Does it? What was happening?

The lights dimmed and the atmosphere chilled. It became cold again. That wasn't a trick. Her friends might be able to fabricate noises, imitate a child's voice, make glasses rattle, but they couldn't change the air temperature, or dim the lights. Or make the mannequin monk scamper around the bar.

The Monk will walk tonight.

Lara stood there, tray in hands, feeling goose bumps all over her. She heard someone laugh again. The cup and the glass on the tray were shaking, ever so gently. She looked down at them trying to steady them. She looked at the oak chair again.

And screamed.

A figure in a dark cowl sat there, in almost the same the pose the man from outside had been. Its hands, grey and gnarled, were gripping the side of the chair. Its head was down on its chest; she couldn't see its face.

Lara didn't want to see its face. She didn't want it to get up. She didn't want it to come towards her with its arms outstretched. But she knew it would. She stared, transfixed, unable to move.

The monk began to lift its head.

Lara dropped the tray. It hit the floor with a resounding crash. Coffee swam around her shoes. She couldn't take her eyes off that hooded head, slowly lifting to look at her. Her skin felt as if it was crawling with lice.

There was nothing, nothing, inside that hood. Just blackness. At first. Then, the eyes gradually formed, except they were not eyes. It was that red luminescence she knew so well from her baby-sitting days. Two red orbs where the eyes should be, bloodshot incandescence, trained on her. Their glare was almost laser-like, emitted from inside the cowl.

Then the devilish laughter again, only it wasn't coming from him.

The monk had now risen to its feet. A sickening feeling of déjà vu swept through her. As it moved towards her, she was transported back four years. Outside Amy's bedroom. The corridor. The monk she experienced in the Gibson's house. Just like this one.

The cloaked evil figure was now shuffling towards her with its grey powdery hands outstretched towards her. They were decaying before her eyes as they advanced. Beneath their grey skin, she could see bones.

Then came the chanting. Just like before.

"La-ra! La-ra!"

Out!

She had to get out.

She had to get away from that ghoulish monk. It was here at last. Monk made manifest. It was going to kill her. Her heart was beating impossibly fast. Any faster and it would burst.

For the second time in her life, Lara Manning ran away.

She raced out to the front lawn, her eyes wild and her hair in disarray. She stood there, gasping painfully, fists clenched, gawping around her. Had it followed her out?

'You cannot leave the hotel, spirit. You are bound inside the place you were generated.'

The gale had dropped as suddenly as it began. The rain had calmed to a slow drizzle.

Lara wouldn't have cared if the storm was still raging. Out here, she was safe.

She was unaware of the sound of sea pounding the shore and the occasional fog horn from the Channel.

Her main thought was escape. Escape the monk.

There was no escape. It would find her wherever she went. It had been in the Gibson's house, now it was here on Herm.

But according to the story, it had always been here. Had it lured her here? To join it?

To be engulfed in the folds of its robes, joining it in its own private Hell for eternity? Was she pre-destined to come to Herm Island and the Monk's Bar, all those years ago?

Was that to be her fate? Yes! Unless she did something. What could she do? What was there to do?

A thought struck her. The church. St. Tugual's.

Sanctuary.

If she sought sanctuary inside a consecrated building, evil couldn't touch her, could it? Then she remembered the other Herm Island Monk story. In the doorway to St. Tugual's was a Monk, buried upright. To deter undesirables from entering the Chapel.

Did Lara want to meet him? Did she really?

She looked at the hotel, the ground floor all lit up. The shutters in the Monk's bar were still open. The till was unguarded. Still things to do before the shift ended. Of the Monk, no sign.

Once upon a time she had left a house with a little girl inside it. To save herself.

Without a thought for Amy. Lara had lived with that for four years.

She had longed for this moment.

That was why she always wanted the Graveyard shift. Her redemption. Never to run away again.

Face your demons, Lara. Be strong. They can't hurt you if you are strong. Go back into the hotel. Finish your shift. You will be proud of yourself.

Whatever that thing was, she would face it. She would challenge it.

Slowly, she retraced her steps to the front door of the hotel. Opened the door and stepped inside.

Waited. Listened. Nothing.

Reception was deserted. Everything was quiet. All the lights were blazing. She walked slowly towards the Monk's Bar, craning her head to see if there was something in the next room. She moved slowly, nervously ready to jump at any sudden sound or movement. Ready to scream. Or run.

The fire in the grate was just glowing embers. Dying as the night began its long stretch until dawn. She thought she saw a face in those embers.

No. Just embers.

There was no sign of it, whatever it was, no sign of anybody. Everything was quiet, normal. No evil laughter, no vibrations, no…visions.

She did all she had to do, secured the till, the bar and locked up.

One thing bothered her. Where was the tray of drinks she had dropped? No sign. Who had cleared it up? Or had she dropped it? Did she imagine it? She was beginning to find her experiences blurring between reality and fantasy.

Otherwise, things couldn't have appeared more normal. The oak chair was empty.

Another reason to feel relief.

Then she suddenly felt an ice block lodge in the pit of her stomach. Freezing tendrils crept outwards over her body.

The monk was not back in his box. He was standing between the sand dunes in the picture. Not laughing this time, but with a wry grin on his face.

You want to play, he appeared to be saying, you reckon you can face me out. And face your fears at the same time. Now's the time, Lara. La-ra! La-ra!

And it was gone from the dunes.

But not gone from the Monk's Bar. Lara knew it was still there, could feel it.

Behind you.

Lara slowly turned round.

It was there.

All the grey flesh had dropped off the hands and now they were skeletal. She felt them crushing her flesh. She cried out in pain. She was pulled towards the Monk. Into its robe. As she was engulfed by the folds of the robe, she felt stifled. Flying eldritch things flew around her head. The screams of the dead echoed through her brain. She lost consciousness, her last sensory impression being the smell of stale earth.

~

Long after the Gibsons had moved out of the house, long after several more families had come and gone, long after the dust emporium had decayed away for good, Lara was standing outside Amy Gibson's bedroom door.

The Monk was making his way down the dark corridor towards her, his vindictive red eyes aglow.

But it could not get into the bedroom. Not with Lara standing sentinel outside the door. Doing her eternal duty. Guarding Amy.

Earning her redemption. For ever and ever, amen.

∾

EDITH AND THE ALIEN

Trying to be as eclectic as possible, I toyed with the idea of including a sci-fi story into the Herm Tale mix. This was the result. It is also probably the closest you will get to a children's story in the collection, although it was not intended to be so. This tale centres around Herm Primary School, whose pupils generally number less than ten. The teacher in the story is entirely fictitious, but the names of some of the children featured in the tale were not entirely grabbed out of thin air. The alien may or may not be fictitious; we will never know...

*T*he Controller's voice rang out in her mind clearly, as the pod circled over the Earth, close to its surface.

"Flug-77602. You have until 14:00 Mehr time to report back. You must make contact with an Earthling. The pod is due back at the landing point at 13:55. If you are not there, it will leave without you. You will be stranded. Repeat. Stranded. Do you understand?"

Flug forwarded her assent mentally. She didn't have to say anything. Her mental message relayed itself back to the Commander.

"We must have your appraisal of the planet's suitability for a Mehrian invasion. As soon as possible."

~

The pod came to rest on Herm Island, at the top of Monku one clear morning in early September. Nobody saw it land, and nobody knew it was there.

Flug hatched out of it, stood up and stretched. As she did so, the pod lifted off and returned from whence it had come.

She watched it go and then looked at her chronometer. The time stood at 08:45. There was a lot to do and not very much time, if she wasn't to be marooned on a strange planet.

She looked all around her to take stock of her situation.

It was very different to her home on Planet Mehr. There was no desert, there were no cities standing in the desert, there were no canals, no crimson sky. Everything was green and blue. Strange large plants with thick brown stems grew out of the ground and reached for the sky with tendril-like appendages, as if they were pointing the way back home.

Large grey rocks lay strewn across the landscape carelessly as if they had been left there by some previous civilization. The sky wasn't red. It was pale blue and white fluffy things were scudding across it. Some sort of force was pulling and pushing Flug. It seemed as if the very air itself was moving.

The deeper blue-ness in the distance also appeared to be moving. It was flecked with white which was in continual motion, there for a moment and then gone, to be replaced by different flecks of white.

Away across a stretch of green was what looked more than a city than anything else in sight. There was a large square building with crenellations. Beneath it, a row of what looked like primitive dwellings.

If Flug was to find signs of life on this strange world, she felt it would be there. She passed through an opening and put a feeler out tentatively on the green part of this peculiar new world in order to make sure it was solid. To her relief, Flug found she could walk on the green surface.

At the other side of the green expanse was another opening and beyond that a track.

Flug concentrated and a word came into her mind.

S…p…i…n…e

The track was called Spine. She made her way towards Spine. She needed to find a lifeform that she could model herself on. If she was to meet and communicate with the inhabitants of this Earth world, she needed to look like them. They would never accept her real appearance. Even if they could see her.

Suddenly Flug thought she had been spotted by the Earthlings.

There was an almighty roaring noise and along the Spine in front of her appeared a monster. It was huge and it made a roaring noise and it was bearing down on her with frightening speed.

Flug stood transfixed in the middle of Spine watching it come at her. Her three little hearts beat wildly and she was sure she was going to be eaten.

Then she realised it was some sort of vehicle. The word 'tractor' came into her mind.

It had large wheels and its pilot sat astride the top of it. He looked like a space warrior in his dark blue uniform and with the cap upon his head. She realised she wasn't going to be eaten. No, she would be crushed beneath one of those large wheels.

Had this warrior on his war machine come for her?

He didn't seem to have seen her. His eyes were focussed on the road ahead. Flug needed to take avoiding action however, or she would be mowed flat by this noisy awesome 'tractor' beast.

She jumped to the side of Spine. Just in time. The beast

thundered past her. Flug looked back and saw it careening down Spine, thin white smoke trailing in its wake.

The warrior on the war machine seemed totally oblivious to her presence. Clearly, he wasn't looking for her. Flug breathed a sigh of relief. It had been a close thing though. Flug had only been on Earth a short time and she had nearly been flattened out of existence.

Still no closer to finding an Earthling whose persona she could adopt, she realised it was important she did so. And soon.

Until she did, there was no way she could infiltrate the Earth's inhabitants' infrastructure and complete her mission. And if she was not back in time, the pod would arrive, register her missing and leave without her. For ever. Stranded on an alien world.

Then came her opportunity. Two Earthlings had appeared in front of her – a Whole-Being and a Halfling. Flug watched them with interest. Both were the female of the species, Flug guessed. The Halfling spoke in a much higher voice than the Whole-Being – maybe a young of the species?

Their appendages were joined. Flug concentrated hard to understand this and words came into her mind.

'Hold…hold…holding hands.'

In earth terms, the Whole-Being was holding the hand of the Halfling.

"Skool…? No! School…" The Halfling was going to School. Whatever School was! She looked at the Halfling. Flug felt she could communicate with her. She increased her pace and overtook them. They couldn't see her in her Mehrian state. But she turned and looked back at the Halfling.

She had brown curly hair that tumbled down either

side of her face, bright alert eyes and a winning smile. She looked happy. Happy to be going to…School. Flug made an on-the-spot decision. The Halfling would be her friend.

She concentrated her mind…concentrated…concentrated…concentrated…

"E-dith. Edith."

The Halfling was known by the name of Edith.

As Flug said the word, she transferred herself into an earth girl, about the same size and age as the Halfling Edith. She imagined herself with straight blonde hair and it was so.

She imagined herself with greeny-grey eyes and it was so. She imagined herself in clothes similar but not identical to the Halfling Edith. And it was so.

Flug looked down at herself. Quite satisfactory.

There they stood. Two earth girls standing, staring at each other, both ready for…School.

Flug realised she had made a mistake. The other girl was looking bemused and startled, possibly by Flug's sudden appearance. "Hello," she said, "My name is…"

She paused.

Her Mehrian name wouldn't do; so Flug was no good. She looked around. There were flowers at the side of the path. Lots of brightly coloured flowers. They had flowers on Mehr, but they weren't as pretty as these. A name popped into her mind.

"I'm Flora," she proclaimed, "I'm a new girl in School."

The Halfling Edith let go of the Whole-Being's hand and skipped happily towards Flug.

"Hello Flora," she said brightly, "Welcome to Herm School."

"Hello E-dith," Flug said and the other girl looked startled all over again.

"How did you know my name?" Edith asked her.

"I heard your...Mum...say it," Flug explained. How easier the Earth words came to her the longer she was on the planet. Because she hadn't heard any such thing; the word 'Mum' came to her from out of the ether and into her mind.

Edith relaxed.

"Well here we are," she said, as they came to a gate. It was the third 'gate' Flug had been through, but the word had only just come to her. On the gate was a notice:

'Free range children. Please shut the gate.'

"This is our school," Edith said as they passed through the portal into the classroom. "Before we go in, I just want to say..."

Edith took both of Flug's hands in hers and looked directly in her eyes.

"We are going to be the best of friends," she said, with a look on her face that Flug read as 'warm' although it was all very alien to her. "I just know it. I'm so glad I met you first. Before anybody else did."

Flug suddenly found herself being hugged by this Earth Halfling. Strangely, she enjoyed the experience somehow and hugged Edith back.

"Let's go and see Miss Oliphant," said Edith, "You'll like her. She's our lovely teacher."

All at once, as they entered the school with pictures on the walls and little desks and tables, Flug realised what 'School' was. It was like her own Learning Factory back on Mehr. Flug's mind went back.

"Pay attention Mehrian juveniles." This was how they were always addressed. The voice, sounding harsh and staccato, always came out of a metallic grating set in the wall. "This morning you are to undertake a project. A

dissertation. You are to plan an invasion of an alien planet. There is a special prize for the best effort. Your work must be written in the best correct Mehrian Grammar with correct Mehrian spelling. There is a real purpose behind this mission. We must find a new world to conquer. A world without red ants that plague, torment and kill us. That is all. You may begin."

The memory of that fateful day was interrupted as Edith tugged on her hand and led Flug up to a Whole-being, another female of the species.

"Good morning, Miss Oliphant," Edith said, "This is Flora. She's the new girl."

Miss Oliphant looked absently at Flug through a pair of what looked like very old-fashioned optical devices.

"New girl? New girl?" she said, consulting a paper book in her hand, "I didn't even know there was a new girl."

Again, Flug's advanced brain picked up the information she needed. She spoke.

"My parents have only just moved to Mehr...I mean Herm," she explained, "I expect my...details will be here tomorrow."

Miss Oliphant shrugged and seemed satisfied.

"Come and sit down," Edith whispered, "There's a spare chair at my table. That's lucky, isn't it?"

But in her mind, Flug was again back on Mehr.

"Mehrian juveniles, I have the results of the dissertation project. The winner is... Flug-77602. Her plan for the invasion of an alien planet in brief was this. To land on the aforesaid planet, adopt the form of the native inhabitant, gather information, assess the planet's suitability for invasion and report back. It is simple but effective and we think it will work. Your prize is to travel through space to just such a planet and carry out the mission you have devised. Well

done Flug-77602. The planet in question is called EARTH. The location on that planet – Herm Island."

"You can sit down Flora," Miss Oliphant was saying.

Flug jerked out of her reverie in surprise, suddenly remembering where she was. This was the…school-room and her new friend Edith was grinning and beckoning her to a seat next to her. Flug somehow stumbled across to it and sat down. She looked at Edith gratefully.

"You're all dozy, aren't you?" Edith said, putting her hand on Flug's. "I'm not surprised. It must all seem very strange and new to you."

Flug could not have agreed more. Miss Oliphant was holding court.

"Right boys and girls. We are off on our nature walk. Did you all bring your packed lunches?"

Everybody in the room called out 'Yes!' except Flug. Packed lunch had not yet reached her vocabulary. How could she have one?

"You didn't know," Edith said, looking at her in concern, "How could you?"

She raised her hand in the air.

"Miss Oliphant, Flora doesn't have a packed lunch. She didn't know about the nature walk. But's it's alright. She can have some of mine. My mum always packs more than enough."

Flug looked at Edith with wide eyes. The word 'kindness' came into her mind. It was totally new to her and it filled her with a strange warmth. She had never experienced it back on Mehr. She was beginning to see Earthling Edith in a totally new light. And liked what she saw very much.

~

The nature walk was very pleasant. In fact, Flug was enjoying it so much, the thought of why she had come to

Earth was rapidly fading from her mind. She loved the companionship of the boys and girls (new words) she was with. She had met Alexei, Amy, Oliver, Max and Beatrice, and found it somehow…life-affirming.

She especially liked being with Edith. And she learned how to laugh.

Laughter was not like anything she had ever encountered on Mehr. It was an exhilarating sensation.

They were walking through the meadow, when the Mehr Commander suddenly contacted Flug.

At first, nothing seemed wrong to Edith. Flug walked quietly by her side, holding her hand, taking great interest in her surroundings.

"It's a pretty island, isn't it?" Edith said, "Don't you think Flora?"

Flora nodded distantly.

"Very pretty," she replied.

"I love living here," Edith went on, "It's so beautiful. You're going to love it too."

"I am sure I will," Flug said, but something in her voice caused Edith to glance anxiously at her. Her voice had become different. It was as if she had something caught in her throat.

In fact, what had happened to Flug had nothing to do with anything in her throat. She was reverting to her Mehrian voice.

The telepathic screen that was being installed in her mind had caused her vision of the outside world on Earth to all but stop.

The fuzziness cleared. Dazzling horizontal flashing lines gave way to a clear view of Mehr Control Centre. The Commander was seated at the console and he looked considerably displeased.

"Flug-77602 – you are in contravention of your orders. You should have made contact some time ago."

"I am sorry Commander," Flug replied and she was shaking in her boots. It didn't do to mess with the Commander. "It took me some time to contact my first Earthling and adopt a similar guise. But I am now fully operational."

"The invasion fleet is on standby Flug-77602; we need information. We require data. If the planet Earth is rich in resources, the invasion will go ahead. We need your input."

"Miss Oliphant," Edith cried out in alarm. "I don't think Flora is very well. Her eyes have gone all glassy and she is speaking...well...gibberish."

The teacher moved over to Flug to find out what was wrong. The other children gathered around, all looking concerned.

"I need more time, Commander," Flug reported back, "I do not have all the data yet. I will report in due course."

"In due course?" thundered the Commander in a voice that made Flug start quaking all over again. Even from the planet Mehr he could reduce her to dust if he so wished. "The pod is due at the location point at 13:55. You must be there in order to return home. But first – you must report. Repeat – YOU – MUST – REPORT!"

The Commander's emotion was being transmitted along with his words right the way through the channels of Space and everything was jangling painfully in Flug's brain.

"She's staggering now, Miss Oliphant," Edith cried. "I think she's going to faint. Please help her."

Miss Oliphant did, by reaching out to stop Flug from falling.

"WE – NEED – TO – KNOW!" The furious voice of the Mehrian Commander continued to jar and splinter Flug's mind. "DO – THE – RESOURCES – ON – EARTH

– MAKE – IT – WORTH – US – PROCEEDING – WITH – THE INVASION? REPORT BACK!"

Relief flooded through Flug as the communication came to an end. But she was still disoriented. She placed her earth-hands on her earth-head and tried to concentrate.

Gradually voices came to her.

"Flora? Are you alright?"

Miss Oliphant.

"Flora. Please say you're OK."

Edith.

Clearly Flug wasn't OK yet, although she thought she would be able to walk. She allowed Miss Oliphant to let her go and she stood still for a moment. Then she staggered to the side of the path and still unable to stand, she fell.

"Oh no. She's fainted, Miss Oliphant," Edith said, "And she's fallen into a clump of stinging nettles."

Flora was aware of an intense stinging on her hands. It hurt. It really hurt. It throbbed, and it was getting worse. It was agony. Her eyes were watering with the pain. She looked down at her earth-hands. They had come up in an ugly red rash. Raised bumps sat high upon her skin. Her breathing altered. It was faster and irregular.

She was going to die here. On Earth. She knew it.

"It's only a stinging nettle," she heard Edith say. "I'll find a dock leaf."

Flug didn't understand.

A stinging nettle. Only a stinging nettle. Dock leaf. It didn't make any sense at all.

She engaged her brain into gear.

Something else did make sense. Flug had been poisoned. The thing called the stinging nettle had put its poison into her. But it hadn't stopped at the earth-skin. It had gone deeper. It had penetrated Flug's Mehrian body. It was racing around what earth people would call her veins and arteries.

It was indeed going to kill her.

The nettle poison was killing her with a slow and agonising death.

It was the same on Mehr with the red ants. Their bite was fatal to Mehrians. It was because of the poison the ants inject you with. And it was here on Earth, in the stinging nettles.

Inside her earth body, on which the poison had caused a mere rash, however painful, her Mehrian body was undergoing a severe allergic reaction to the poison. Her Mehrian mind managed to form a word…

"F…O…R…M…I…C…"

On Earth, the poison was called formic.

Formic was killing Flug. She would never return to Mehr. The formic would finish her. She would not be able to warn Mehr. And if they did not hear from her, they would invade. And they too would be poisoned by the formic.

She heard Edith's voice again.

"Here we are Flora," she was saying. "I have found some dock leaves. I have loads of them. They will take the sting away, I promise."

Edith was rubbing something against her earth-skin. Something…green. It was cool and it took away the sting of the nettles. But inside her earth body, her Mehrian body was still in agony. Twisting and writhing with pain. Going into death-throes, Flug was sure of it.

What would happen to her Flora earth-body, Flug wondered, when her Mehrian body died inside?

Edith, and now her friends, were still applying the cooling green leaves to her earth-skin. And something wonderful started to happen.

A good feeling was spreading through her. Not just through her earth-body but through her Mehrian body as well. The formic was going; it was disappearing. The strange green leaves, the 'dock' leaves contained an antidote for the formic.

Flug knew what she had to do. Firstly, she had to get away and report back to the Commander. She had things to tell him. Important things. Things that might save Mehrian people from dying.

Earth would be good to invade. For the dock-leaf plant alone. They could transport it back to Mehr and no Mehrian would ever die from the red ant bites again.

"I have to go," she said to Edith.

"Go? Where?" Edith said, "You can't go off on your own. It's not allowed."

Flug was already backing away from the group of schoolchildren, who seemed quite unaware of the drama unfolding between Edith and their new school-friend Flora.

"Flora! Come back!"

Flug disappeared. Of course, she had transferred herself back into her Mehrian state. No-one could see her. She sent her mind over the assembled company at the nature walk, including Miss Oliphant, so that they should forget that Flora ever existed, which of course, she didn't really.

Only Edith remembered. She stood, looking puzzled and upset at the loss of her new friend. Somehow, she had withstood Flug's 'forget-me' vibe. It was the bond of friendship that had done it.

Flug called the Commander.

"About time!" was his only comment. He awaited her report. Flug could feel his impatience; it crackled in her

mind. For some reason, she couldn't speak.

"Do we invade?" the Commander stormed, "We are ready. Fifteen minutes and we can eliminate the entire population of Earth. Without damage to the resources. If the resources are suitable for our needs, we will go ahead. Please give your report Flug-77602. DO WE INVADE?"

Flug looked back at her new friends.

Alexei was watching a particularly pretty butterfly, Amy studiously counted the petals on a buttercup, Beatrice was making a daisy chain, Oliver watched a ladybird climb to the top of a blade of grass and Max had fallen asleep. Miss Oliphant was gazing in a kindly fashion on her little flock. The Herm sun reigned supreme and warmed the earth. It was all so serene and peaceful.

In that instant, Flug realised that her time on earth had imbued her with new feelings. Kindness and compassion. She looked at Edith. Tears were streaming down the little girl's face.

In that moment, Flug made her decision.

"Flug-77602 reporting to Mehrian Commander. There are no resources on Earth of interest to Mehr," her mind sent into Space to Mehr, "The planet is barren and devoid of anything useful. Do not invade Earth! Repeat! Do not invade Earth!"

"We copy, Flug-77602. The pod is returning for you. Please be at the appointed place. Out!"

Flug sighed with relief. And reappeared in human form.

"Flora!" Edith cried and hugged her so hard, Flug thought she would break her outer human frame. "You came back!"

"Yes, but I haven't got long," Flug said, glancing over at Miss Oliphant, who was gently waking the sleeping Max.

"Edith. This is going to be hard for you to understand. I am not even going to try to explain it in words. I am going to think my story into your mind. Ready?"

"Ready," Edith replied, looking a little worried.

Flug's brow creased as she concentrated. She telepathically imparted to Edith how she had come to Earth from Mehr in a pod and adopted her human frame. She didn't say why or anything about the proposed invasion. She just said that she was curious about what the Earth might be like. As Flug's thoughts tumbled into Edith's mind from her own, Edith's eyes were tight shut.

When Flug had finished, Edith opened her eyes, with a look of amazement on her face.

"My friend is an alien," she breathed in wonder.

Flug glanced at her chronometer.

"I have to go. I mustn't miss the pod. Edith, it has been so lovely to meet you."

"And you too."

They held hands briefly, then Flug was away down Spine. As she went, she changed herself back into her Mehrian form. All Edith saw was her new friend lightly dissolve into the air. She felt a sense of sadness, but she silently wished Flora a safe journey home to her own planet.

For many years to come, Edith would gaze out of her window up at the skies, looking into Space, wondering where in the galaxy, her friend Flora was. Some nights, she thought she saw Flora's face up there, framed in stars.

⁓

In the pod, Flug uncurled her tiny Mehrian hand.

She was clutching a little sprig of greenery. It was a tiny shred of the plant called 'dock-leaf'.

Already Flug's mind was formulating the chemical structure of the antidote to 'formic'.

It would save thousands of Mehrian lives.

~

THE SISTERS' LAST RESTING
PLACE

Vampires on Herm? Well why not? There are already dragons, witches, fairies, pirates, ghosts and Neolithic spirits? And where better to place a couple of vampire sisters than in the log cabins just off the Spine Road towards the South Cliffs. I believe I once saw the Graves sisters in the Mermaid courtyard (I convinced myself that it was them) and that was where the idea for the story came from – two ladies wearing shades and sun hats and looking distinctly uncomfortable in the sunshine and heat came in trying to find the most shaded area. Both looked to my writer's imagination, a little 'odd'. Readers, I give you Sepulchra and Morticia Graves. Oh by the way, if you know your history of the island, you'll know there were also wallabies on Herm (really).

A Herm November night.
Pitch black and icy cold. Even the sky wore a cowl. Ilsa Strofeld pulled her coat more tightly around her as she struggled down the drive against the freezing blast that was doing its best to blow her back up. It had been a brisk walk from the log cabin where she was staying along the Spine Road.

She passed the cottages that overlooked the large expanse of meadow land, passed St Tugual's (a dark forbidding arch, Ilsa thought, I have no intention of venturing in there) and then down the drive. The trees adopted the cutting wind and turned it into the Herm night song.

There would be a warming fire in the Mermaid Tavern. It was kept banked up, especially this time of year, for the residents. There were always a few hardy self-catering visitors, who like herself, were drawn to the island when it was out of season.

A sudden overhead flapping startled her. Too late in the day for any of the island's birdlife, with the exception perhaps of an occasional owl; a fluttering of bats maybe. Sure enough, two raggedy bats circled and dipped, trying to maintain momentum against the wind, seen clearly because they were even blacker than the night's sky.

Ilsa chuckled to herself. She wondered if tonight's storyteller would incorporate bats into his tale of terror. If not, he would learn soon enough.

At the bottom of the drive, she turned right past the gift shops and Mermaid cottages and turned into the courtyard of the Tavern. The smoky smell of grilled steak pervaded the air, quickening her appetite.

The Mermaid was buzzing, surprisingly full for the time of year, and the staff busied themselves serving residents and guests alike; a party had come over by boat from Guernsey for a late session and to hear the storyteller spin his yarn for this unyielding November night.

When Ilsa's turn at the bar came, she ordered a pint of the seasonal Winter's brew and a steak, rare. The beer was dark, almost reddish in colour, and tasted of hops, raisins and Christmas spices. It reminded her of the Christmas markets at home. She sat herself by the 'Staff Only' door, with a good view of the fire. She felt warmed by the mere sight of the flames. Sipping her beer again, she took a look around.

People were happy, eating, drinking and talking, often loudly laughing.

Trevor Cross, Guernsey author and performance poet, was to tell the story 'Vampires on Herm – the Graves Sisters – a true story'. A must for Ilsa, who loved stories about vampires. This one in particular excited her keen curiosity.

Trevor Cross was holding forth at the bar, a tankard of ale in his hand. He was an enormous man, in excess of six foot with a leonine mane of bushy blonde hair and a moustache to match. This was a man who, amongst his areas of expertise, numbered the myths and folklore of the Channel Islands, including the 'ghosties and ghoulies and the long-leggedy beasties'. He had also been known to take in the occasional vampire or werewolf.

He certainly looked the part – academic, mythologian, author, poet. All of these within a large jovial frame. Ilsa thought there might be hidden depths of horror inside the man, rarely seen in his performances. On some dark, sinister night however, this might be revealed to an unwary travelling companion – unless such a person was prepared.

As Ilsa was.

The big man rose to his feet, rattled a fork on a plate and cleared his throat. It was time. His large frame moved effortlessly to the fire, where he took up his traditional stance for ghost-story tellers, his back to it. An expectant hush settled over the company.

"Ladies and gentlemen," he began in his big booming voice. "Friends, and…fellow vampire hunters."

A nervous laugh broke out from some areas in the room.

"Come with me if you will on a vampire hunt. A hunt

that took place on this very island of Herm not too many years ago. Vampires on Herm, I hear you cry? Impossible!"

He lowered his voice.

"Friends. I have documented evidence from one of my forbears who led the hunt for two well-established vampires who existed here on Herm for several seasons. I say 'existed' and not 'lived'; those of you familiar with the tradition, know only too well that vampires are of the species 'undead' and cannot be said to be 'living'. No, my friends, they existed and pursued their foul and evil practice of preying on the living and sucking their blood.

"Their names were Sepulchra and Morticia Graves and they were sisters. These were their given names because of course, their Eastern European names were difficult to spell what with all those consonants and very few vowels, and impossible to pronounce. So Sepulchra and Morticia they became. Apposite forenames for a pair of dark sisters and an appropriate surname to boot.

"Sepulchra was the elder by two years. A thin willowy figure, she was much taller than her sister. Morticia was not as slender and although you wouldn't call her fat, she had more meat on her than Sepulchra. She also had more colour, more redness in her cheeks. She fed well, we must presume."

Another uncertain ripple of laughter.

"The Graves sisters first came to Guernsey from Transylvania on flight TR666, Balkan Airlines, one of the very few airlines that flew into Guernsey Airport late in the evening. They disappeared quickly after the immigration procedures, but when the aircraft was boarded, it was found that the cabin crew were disabled and extremely anaemic, bearing strange puncture marks in their necks. They were transported to the Princess Elizabeth

Hospital on Guernsey for immediate blood transfusions. All the other passengers on the flight had mysteriously disappeared.

"How did Sepulchra and Morticia fare on Herm Island? I'm coming to that next. In fact, I'm taking you to the log cabins in the wood just beyond Manor Village…"

Trevor waved his arms in front of him, as if inviting a dramatized flashback.

~

It was a dull day in October and the log cabins lay sleepily nestled amongst the trees. A few late insects were still buzzing around what remained of the Summer flowers, but apart from that, the atmosphere was still and sombre.

Just the way the sisters liked it. Free of interfering busybodies and especially away from the Hunters. In particular, the man they had come to loathe and fear with all their Undead being – Robert de la Croix.

"Come away from the window dear," said Sepulchra.

"I don't know why you're worrying dear," Morticia, her sister replied, "There's absolutely nobody about."

"It's not people I'm worried about dear," said Sepulchra, "You'll get blisters from the daylight."

Morticia sighed.

"I wish there were more people about. I haven't had a proper feed since the flight."

"No," agreed Sepulchra, "We had to leave the pilot alone. We could never have landed the plane ourselves."

"Are there not even any fresh mice left?" Morticia asked.

"I'm afraid not dear," Sepulchra told her, "We shared the last one walking up the drive."

"Goodness, that hill," moaned Morticia, "By the time I got to the top, every breath was like a stake through the heart."

She sat down, puffed out by the memory.

"Oh Sepulchra," she cried, "It was a mistake coming here. Don't you wish we were back in Transylvania?"

"No dear, I most definitely do not," her sister said firmly, "Things were getting too dangerous for us there. Why, it was getting so that there were more Hunters than there were Undead. No, I definitely think this Herm Island place is right for us. It's so isolated."

"Too isolated," Morticia complained, "There's not going to be enough food."

"Look, as soon as the sun is low in the sky, we'll pop our coats on and go foraging. There must be some wildlife on the island surely. Deer maybe, or…"

"Remember Australia?" Morticia broke in, "Sumptuous repasts to be had there." She sighed. "Those tender young wallabies were succulent. Sepulchra! Do you think there are wallabies on Herm?"

"Don't be silly dear. Herm is a Channel Island. I don't think you'll find any wallabies here."

"Shame," said Morticia, "I could do with a nice succulent wallaby…"

At sundown, they got themselves ready for their walk.

"Don't forget your shades Morticia, you know what the light of dusk does to your eyes."

They left the log cabin unlocked. There was no need to lock it. If one of the Hunters should find it, they'd just pin a crucifix or a sprig of garlic to the door. The sisters wouldn't be able to get back in anyway.

They wandered hand in hand down the Spine road, the taller Sepulchra vigilant, always on the lookout for a

Hunter, but the eager-eyed Morticia eyeing the lights that began to twinkle in Guernsey across the water, where there would be plenty of people wandering around in the twilight. Plenty of food. A late-night snack after the pubs closed.

As they approached the bottom of the Spine Road, Morticia felt her sister's hand tighten on hers. She stopped abruptly. Morticia looked at her with alarm.

"What's up dear?"

A choking sound was coming from Sepulchra's throat and her eyes were wide. She let go of Morticia's hand and pointed.

"Look!" She could barely say the word.

Morticia looked and her breath caught in her throat when she saw what Sepulchra had seen. A few yards in front of them stood a post and at the top of that post was a cross, constructed out of four cross pieces, each pointing in a different direction.

A sign at the top of this structure read 'Robert's Cross.'

"Goodness!" Morticia cried out. "Is he here?"

"He can't be," Sepulchra said, "We left him behind in Transylvania."

She was referring to the renowned hunter Robert de la Croix, who was the main reason they had fled their native homeland.

"Let's not go near there, Sepulchra," begged Morticia, "Just in case."

"Of course not," the other agreed, "Let us head across the grass. To that large mound with the rocks on top."

"Yes. My goodness." Morticia gazed upwards in awe. "It looks like a throne. Whoever sat up there must have commanded the island."

"It would have been a fitting throne for our Master,"

Sepulchra proclaimed, "Had he not been destroyed by that German Hunter, Professor Van…"

"Don't speak his name, dear," Morticia cut in, "Just the sound of it gives me the willies."

She shuddered and pulled her coat more tightly around her.

"Anyway, our bloodline has not been destroyed," Sepulchra said, "Our race has survived. Even though there are still Hunters. That is why I thought this island would be good for us. Our resting place."

"Our last resting place," added Morticia, "No more running away. Unhindered by the likes of Robert de la Croix."

Sepulchra's eyes suddenly widened. She gripped Morticia's arm, not as fiercely as before.

"Look Sister," she urged, "Rabbits!"

~

"Can you imagine the sisters' joy?" Trevor Cross paused for dramatic emphasis and his eyes circled the room to see the effect he was having. His audience was hanging on his every word, breathless, waiting for him to continue.

He didn't disappoint.

"The rabbits were the start. A plentiful source of them on the common. Then there were the pheasants. Fair game, if you'll pardon the pun. But soon, the sisters were craving what they loved most. Human blood.

"They didn't want to touch the island folk for some reason. Maybe they felt indebted to them, for letting them stay there and get on with their business. Because, make no mistake, the residents knew of them. Two strange pale ladies who lived in one of the log cabins. The sisters paid their way. They kept themselves to themselves. I suppose they didn't want to upset their hosts."

Trevor paused and quaffed his pint. Ilsa was amused to notice that his whiskers had acquired a frothy adornment.

"Foreign backpackers were the sisters' favourite repast. Not only did they taste more like the provender back home, but they didn't seem to raise much of a hue and cry when they went missing. It worked quite well. The old copper-mine workings were a suitable disposal chute for the leftovers. Sepulchra didn't need as much sustenance anyway. She was tall but she was as thin as a rake and kept herself that way. Morticia, being plumper, had a much greater appetite. When she started to get greedier, Sepulchra put on her diet. It was as simple as that. Morticia complained but Sepulchra's will was always the stronger."

He paused.

"Barman! More beer!" he cried. "The telling of how these two weird and evil sisters were caught requires a re-charging of the tankard, if you please!"

The barman obliged.

Trevor accepted the tankard, took a large swig and began the close of his tale.

"What the sisters didn't know was that Robert de la Croix had tracked them down once again. He picked up their trail in Transylvania quite easily not long after they had supped their way across Europe with the in-flight meal the cabin stewards hadn't provided with smiles on their faces...Once in Guernsey, it didn't take Robert long to track them to Herm..."

Trevor stared sombrely over the top of his glass.

"Poor Sepulchra and Morticia. The decision to take a walk that day was to be the nail in their collective coffin."

～

It was a day late in the Summer. The weather had alternated between rain and hot sunshine, both bad for the sisters, so they had spent a lot of time in the cabin. They played games – 'Operation' with the carcass and bones of a dead rabbit, 'Pick-up Sticks' although they had to stop that because Morticia got upset by their pointed ends, 'Transylvanian Monopoly' although Morticia always lost and never got to pass Go and get to the Blood Bank.

"I think a walk is in order dear," Sepulchra said. "The sun's gone in. We'll wander down to the shop and see if we can get some blood oranges."

"As long as it doesn't rain," Morticia said. "You know how running water gives us nasty blisters."

It was a relief for them both to be out after such a long time indoors. So much so, they didn't notice the build-up of altocumulus clouds high over the north end of the island.

They walked past the cottages, the same path Ilsa Strofeld was to take many years later.

As they passed the entrance to St. Tugual's, Sepulchra said: "I hate that dark forbidding arch."

"You wouldn't find me dead in there," Morticia added.

They both shuddered, pulled their coats around them more tightly and ambled down the drive in a carefree manner.

A figure carrying a mallet and a wooden stake appeared from the arch and followed them down.

They turned left at the bottom of the drive and made their way past the Mermaid.

A second figure, also carrying the deadly equipment, stepped out of the Mermaid courtyard. The two men followed the sisters, one grim purpose in both their minds. As they passed Fisherman's cottage, a third man with exactly the same accoutrements, stepped out from the narrow path. Robert de la Croix was taking no chances. Now he had found the Graves sisters, he had no intention of letting them get away. He had assembled a veritable posse of Hunters, all equipped with the tools of their trade – stakes to penetrate the hearts of the vampire women and mallets to drive them home.

At the exact point when Sepulchra realised they were being followed, thunder sounded overhead.

"It's going to rain!" cried Morticia fearfully. "Rain, Sepulchra!"

"That's the least of our problems dear," Sepulchra said, more calmly than she felt, "There are three Hunters behind us."

Morticia looked back. Sepulchra looked forward. Three more Hunters had appeared on the path ahead of them. One of them was tall and broad and sported a large bushy beard.

"Robert de la Croix," breathed Sepulchra. "He's caught up with us at last."

Morticia squealed as the first drop of storm rain hit her forehead. Her skin immediately blistered.

"What'll we do Sepulchra? Think of something!"

"The beach!" cried Sepulchra shrilly. "Maybe there are caves, rocks. Maybe we can hide. If not…"

"What?"

"You know what. The rain will hurt. It'll scald and sting. But it's the only way to escape those Hunters' stakes. If we stay free long enough."

They scampered down the slope onto Bear Beach. The rain began in earnest. Morticia gave a little scream every time a raindrop hit her bare skin, but Sepulchra, made of sterner stuff, took the painful stings in silence.

"I can't see any caves dear," said Morticia.

"I don't think there are any caves dear," said Sepulchra.

Morticia let fly with a good old Transylvanian obscenity. Meanwhile three of the Hunters had reached the top of the steps and the other three were scrambling down the bank.

"To the sea!" screamed Sepulchra. "It's our only chance."

Hand in hand, the two sisters hobbled as fast as they could to the sea's edge. The incoming tide lapped over the feet and they both howled in pain.

"It's set my gout off," Morticia complained.

Two raggedy figures stood miserably in the sea, hand in hand, flinching in agony from the stinging rain.

The six Hunters were striding across the beach towards them.

Robert de la Croix stopped and looked. Something was happening to the weird evil sisters. Somehow, they were diminishing.

"RUN!" he cried, "We're losing them!"

The Hunters got to where the sisters had been standing. Their clothes remained.

Of the two vampire women – nothing!

Robert de la Croix cursed and trampled the remains of the rags underfoot.

Well! They've gone, haven't they? He'd chased them to the water, hadn't he?

It was his doing, wasn't it? He should claim the credit, shouldn't he?

They had destroyed the Graves sisters; even if he and his faithful fellow Hunters had to embellish the story a little – twist the truth just a tad.

~

Ilsa waited until Trevor had finished his beer, wiped

his mouth, belched noisily, laughing at himself for doing it and made his way to the door of the Mermaid. She rose silently, finished her drink and carefully placed her glass down on the table. Unnoticed by anyone, she slipped out of the door after him. He was making his way along the path towards the drive. Ilsa could see the tall, lumbering shape of him, silhouetted against the light from the harbour. She easily caught him up.

"Mr De La Croix?" she challenged him.

He stopped and looked down at her, puzzlement on his face.

"Cross is the name," he said, "Trevor Cross."

"But you were once de la Croix. Or at least your family was. That vampire hunter you were speaking of…Robert de la Croix…a relative from a generation long since gone, surely. By the way, congratulations on your oratory. It was a very impressive performance."

Ilsa knew that Trevor was the sort of man who would succumb to a little bit of flattery and she was right. A complacent grin spread across his face.

"Well thank you, I am glad you appreciated it, Miss…"

"Strofeld, Ilsa Strofeld," she said to him.

"You see Miss Strofeld, I keep the de la Croix bit quiet, for obvious reasons. I mean, my forbear was a Hunter, you understand. He tracked down and destroyed vampires. You never know when you are going to meet one of those filthy creatures again, do you? Some descendant may be bent on revenge, you never know."

"It's entirely possible," Ilsa replied.

"Are you walking up the drive, Miss Strofeld?"

"I am indeed. I am booked into one of the log cabins."

"Damned coincidence. So am I."

Ilsa knew that. She had checked.

By the time they reached the Spine road, Trevor Cross looked truly out of condition and was panting heavily. The numerous pints of beer he had consumed through the evening had obviously taken their toll. Ilsa felt spry, alive.

Ready for what was to come. At the log cabins, they stopped.

"Well," Ilsa said, "Time to say goodnight."

"Oh, not necessarily," Trevor said, "I've got a nice bottle of cognac in my cabin. Surely you have time for a nightcap? We could get to know each other a little better."

"I think not," Ilsa said, "I have to get a flight back home tomorrow."

Ilsa had anticipated his next move. He lurched in towards her, a lecherous leering grin on his face.

"Well, maybe just a goodnight kiss then?" he pleaded, "You are a very attractive girl."

His arms were suddenly around her and his face crushing up against hers. Ilsa was repulsed by the feel of the bushy whiskers on her face and the smell of beer and garlic on his breath. Especially the garlic. But she managed to endure it, although her stomach was screaming out to vomit. It was all part of the plan.

He pushed his tongue in her mouth and probed. It was all she could do to stop herself crying out in disgust. His mouth went to the side of her face and he started nibbling on her ear lobe. This was Ilsa's chance. His neck was exposed to her mouth.

She felt a tingling sensation inside her mouth at the top of her gums at each side. She ran her tongue over each of the fangs that had grown there and felt inner satisfaction. Her blood was coursing around her body, strong and vibrant.

She used her right hand to push away Trevor Cross's

hair and felt for his neck with her lips. He murmured with pleasure and pulled her closer to him. His left hand began to pull at her clothes.

It was so easy for Ilsa. Her fangs slid effortlessly into the side of his neck.

He screeched and froze, suddenly realising he was in trouble. But Ilsa's first taste of his blood strengthened her and weakened him. Her mouth closed over the two puncture marks and she began to suck, tasting the rich red blood as it flowed into her mouth and down her throat.

Ilsa was not greedy. There were others relying on the life-blood of Trevor Cross, aka Trevor de la Croix, aka descendant of Robert de la Croix, Hunter, the man responsible for hunting down her Aunt Sepulchra and her Aunt Morticia. She fed on him until she felt his consciousness going. She let him go and he fell comatose to the ground. His mouth was frothing again, although not with beer this time. A trickle of blood ran down his neck from each puncture-hole. His eyes had revolved in their sockets until only the whites showed. Ilsa took a few steps away from him and called softly into the dark night air.

"Aunt Seppy," she cried, "Aunt Morty."

There was an almost silent pause broken only by the now distant wind away out to sea. Then came the welcome flapping sound and two bats appeared out of apparently nowhere.

"Hello," Ilsa greeted them warmly. "It's nearly time."

The bats sat on the wooden fence, watching and waiting. Ilsa found Cross's key and unlocked his cabin. Then she dragged his body inside, easily, in spite of his bulk. Some deft work with a couple of kitchen utensils resulted in her emerging from the cabin with a large saucepan filled with a dark red liquid. The bats stirred expectantly as Ilsa carried it over to them. She placed it on the ground in front of them.

The bats rose in the air, fluttered their wings and flew down to the rejuvenating feast their niece had prepared for them. Ilsa left the happy slurping sounds and went inside to clear up and partake of a final little supper for herself.

When she went back outside, she was greeted by a tall slender woman and a shorter plumper one. Her beloved aunts.

"Hello dear," Sepulchra said.

"Hello dear," Morticia said.

Ilsa ran to them and gave them both a hug.

"As promised!" she said, "You're back."

"Many thanks dear," Sepulchra said.

"We owe you so much," Morticia added.

"You owe me nothing," Ilsa said, "Family honour is satisfied, revenge is ours, the last member of that accursed Hunter family, Trevor de la Croix is…fixed. For good. I used his own weapons against him. He was carrying two wooden stakes and a mallet."

"So, he was a Hunter too?" Morticia gasped.

"He liked to think he was," Ilsa said, "But I don't think he ever thought he'd actually meet a vampire." She smiled darkly, showing the traces of blood that had crusted at the corners of her mouth, "But he was wrong, wasn't he?"

The three of them cackled together.

"But Aunties," Ilsa said, her tone of voice changing, "Won't you come back home with me? I don't like the thought of you staying here on this lonely island, as idyllic as it seems to be. What will you do for food? You can't live on rabbits, pheasants and foreign backpackers forever."

"Well we haven't started on the Herm residents yet?"

Morticia said, eyeing her sister eagerly.

But Sepulchra slapped her on the wrist.

"And neither will we," she said sternly, "They've been very kind to us. Very hospitable. We will not dine on the residents of Herm." Then her eyes gleamed. "But across the water there is an island ripe for cultivation."

"Guernsey?" her sister ventured.

"No," Sepulchra said, "Sark!"

~

A WALK BEFORE THE WEDDING

The Blucher family's time on Herm Island is well documented, and Princess Radziwell's Walk, in the White House Hotel grounds, bears testament to it. I wanted to place a modern-day bride on that walk on the morning of her wedding. What if she had doubts about her marriage? What if she were to meet...? Perhaps it's time to read the story. The horrendous wedding planner in this tale bears no resemblance to any real person, although Herm Island has played host to many weddings, presumably some with their own wedding planners. Neither of course, do any of the other characters, except maybe the strange lady that our bride-to-be meets on her walk.

The formidable woman stood like a colossus at the end of Herm Harbour. Her blonde hair was close-cropped and her square jaw determined. She was barking instructions to everybody within hearing range and clearly did not expect to be argued with.

Hilary Turnbull, self-styled wedding-organiser extraordinaire, was all set to deliver to the Ponsonby-Sloane family of Guernsey 'a blissful and remarkable wedding day that will live on in the memory forever', the whole event to take place upon Herm Island.

She was organising the newly-arrived consignment of flowers that had almost depleted the supply of every single florist on Guernsey. It was being unloaded from the launch, into assorted tractors and trailers, some on their way to the Mermaid Tavern, some to the marquee especially erected for the occasion and some to the church.

Hilary rammed her mobile phone to her ear and yelled into it.

"Desmond. Can you send a runner down please to pick up the buttonholes? And make sure Lisle checks all the video links are working."

An elaborate video-system would relay the ceremony from St Tugual's Church to huge screens in the Mermaid forecourt and the marquee in the gardens of the White House Hotel. The wedding banquet was laid out in the Conservatory restaurant and the neighbouring Ship Inn, whilst lesser mortals would be treated to a lavish buffet in the marquee. So, whilst partaking of the vol-au-vents, cocktail sausages and salmon and cucumber sandwiches, they would be able to watch the speeches on the large screen there.

"I don't care if he says he's done it; get him to do it again. You know what he's like. Do it Desmond. Just do it."

She snapped her phone off and dialled another number.

"Candice? How are things in the kitchen? Pimms, champagne and bucks fizz ready? Is Chef happy? Are you sure? Why am I asking? Candice...darling...because I can hear someone shouting. And nobody is to swear, however stressed they get. I don't care what language they swear in, Candice; nobody is to swear at all. For pity's sake, Candice, this is a wedding."

She snapped her phone shut again, totally unaware of the bemused looks she was receiving from the crew of the boat and other workers. She jabbed another number into the keypad.

"Francis, what time is the boat arriving with the groom's party? Well keep him away from the hotel. You know what he's like. You don't know what he's like? Well Francis, he's just likely to try and pop in and say hello to the bride, that's what he's like! I will not have wedding etiquette breached under any circumstances. It's bad luck for them to meet before the ceremony on the wedding-day, that's why. Just be an angel and get him into the Mermaid Cottages where the rest of the groom's close party are. Don't let him go anywhere near the hotel gardens, let alone into the White House itself."

Snap. Multiple jabbing. Press to ear.

"Phoebe, are you still covering hotel reception? Is everything quiet there? Look, will you pop up to room 3, where they're dressing the bride? Have a listen outside the door, would you? Make sure everything is quiet in there. If there's a disturbance, tap on the door, stick your head in and ask if everything is alright. Because I am expecting an outburst from that horrendous woman. You know what she's like. I'm not talking about the bride. She's a mousy little thing. It's the bride's mother. Mrs Dolores Ponsonby-Sloane. She's a bully, that woman. You can burst in if you have to, Phoebe, you have my authority. Now do as you're told. Don't argue. I'm telling you, Phoebe. Yes. Me, Phoebe. Just do it!"

Snap. Even more furious relentless pressing of mobile phone keypad.

"Fritz? How's things at the church? Now remember, the seating plan is inviolable. Have you memorised it? What do you mean, more or less? Yes, I do expect you to recognise all the close family members by sight and direct them to their seats. Anyway, you've got the ushers to help you, haven't you? Let them do the work. Just be on hand. They should be there already; in Sea Holly Cottage relaxing, until it's time for them to start ushing. Are they there?"

A pause whilst Hilary's eyes did several manic panoramic back-and-forth sweeps across her domain.

"They are? Good. With their hip flasks. They have one each? Yes, I'm sure they're getting along very merrily. Get in there, Fritz! Make sure they don't get too happy. You know what they're like. I don't care if they're built like night-club bouncers and look as if they could turn mean. See to it. Are the cameramen in their positions? What about the Reverend? He's alright, is he? He's singing to himself. OK. as long as he doesn't have a hip flask as well."

Snap. Dialling.

"Vernon. The thingummies for the bridal buggy are on their way. They all have whassanames, you know, whatdoyoumacallits. Oh, Vernon, of course you know what I mean. Don't antagonise me. I mean attachments, so they should easily fit to the sides of the buggies without any danger of them falling off. Is it absolutely clean inside the buggy? No dirt or dust or mud on any of the seats? If there is a single mark on the bride's dress when she arrives, heads will roll. Is the driver there? What's his name? Tom? Put him on." A pause. "Tom? This is Hilary Turnbull, wedding-organiser..." She almost said 'extraordinaire' but stopped herself, just in time.

"Tom? Hello Tom. Now are you sure there are enough seats in the buggy for the whole bridal party? That's...the bride, the bride's mother and father, two adult bridesmaids and four children – two little bridesmaids and two little pageboys...nine in all. What's that? Well if the father of the bride can't ride...what do you say...shotgun with you, then he'll have to walk up... No, I do not want the children sitting on the bridesmaids' laps, they'll crumple their dresses. No, I don't think a tractor with a cart following behind is a good idea either. Can you put Vernon back on please?

"Vernon. Can you see the buggy? Are you standing near it? You are. Good. Well take a good look inside. Realistically, is there enough room for nine persons? I'm sorry, Vernon, 'with a bit of a squeeze' is not good enough. The bride's father and the two page boys can walk up. Yes, you'll have to tell them, and you can walk up with them. I can't help your gammy leg, Vernon, just do it!"

She snapped her phone shut. Something suddenly momentous caught her attention and her square jaw atrophied in horror. Not believing what she was seeing, she furiously stabbed in a number. An infuriating voice informed her that the person was unable to answer the phone at the moment. She tried again. Same result. And again. At last, her call was answered.

"Phoebe!" she thundered, "Have you taken leave of your senses? What do you mean, what do I mean? The bride has just walked out of the hotel. What do you mean, you know? You should have stopped her, Phoebe....because she's the bloody bride and she's getting married in less than two hours. She should be getting into her trousseau. Now get out there, get after her and get her back. No. Don't ring off. Stay on the line. I want you to stay with me until our sheep is safely back in the fold. Are you on your way? Good."

Anxiously, she scanned the hotel garden for a sign of Phoebe.

"Phoebe, did you do what I said? Did you listen outside the room? You did. And? There were raised voices. I knew it. She was having a row with her mother. That bullying harridan. Standing over her? The bride was in tears? A fine thing, for a girl to be crying on her wedding morning. Where are you now Phoebe? You're outside the Hotel. I think I knew that Phoebe, but whereabouts outside the hotel? Can you see the bride? She went left Phoebe. No, not towards the Mermaid, the other way. Towards the marquee. I can't see her now. She walked along the path and she's disappeared behind the marquee. Hurry up, Phoebe. What do you mean, no sign of her? Find the bride, Phoebe. Find the bloody bride. Just do it!"

~

In fact, Isobel Ponsonby-Sloane, the disappearing bride-in-question, had slipped into the hotel garden, walked past the swimming pool and recliners and found the sign pointing intriguingly to 'Princess Radziwell's Walk – for Hotel Guests only'.

Tears were drying on her face as she climbed the walk; she was also ruminating on the fact that a girl's wedding day was supposed to be the happiest day of her life. Happening to remark to her mother that she wondered if she was doing the right thing, Issy didn't realize what a storm she would unleash. Of course, her mother would say it was the right thing to do. Her mother had long wanted access into the Guernsey High Society In-Crowd and if marrying off her daughter to Guy Le Prevost was part of the entry-card to that elite, then what right did her tiresome daughter have to question if she was doing the right thing?

How Dolores Ponsonby-Sloane, her nostrils flaring and eyes bursting with iodine-deficient thyroid intensity had paraded around, like a wild boar in an afternoon tea-room.

"You are just the end, Isobel." Always Isobel, never Issy, when she was in full battle mode. "The end. Guy Le Prevost is the most eligible bachelor on Guernsey, he has asked you to marry him and you are having doubts. On your wedding day. I really don't understand you."

"You never have," snapped Issy. "What if I've discovered I don't love him after all?"

"Then start loving him," her mother riposted. Issy thought that she must look like one of the fabled Herm dragons; she wouldn't have been surprised to see sulfurous flames spurt out of her nostrils.

"He's a lot older than me, Mum," Issy pointed out, "Maybe I made a mistake."

"Made a...?" Dolores was now looking apoplectic. Purple veins stood out on her forehead. "Now listen to me, you foolish, ungrateful child."

She reads too many Victorian novelists, Issy thought.

"Today is your wedding day and you are going to marry Guy Le Prevost whether you like it or not. Deal with it!"

"But..."

"No buts!" her mother interrupted, leaning over her and smelling heavily of garlic, onion and alcohol.

Issy's stomach heaved and she suddenly felt she badly needed some air.

"Where are you going?" Dolores screeched as Issy made for the door.

Issy didn't dignify the question with a reply. She heard her mother scream it out again, as she ran down the stairs towards reception.

～

The going up the slope was getting tougher and steeper now as she approached the top of Princess Radziwell's walk, probably one of the highest points on the island. Bees hung lazily about the blossom on the bushes on either side of the path. The sounds of the wedding preparation got more remote the higher she climbed. She liked that. It was good to be away from it all, especially her domineering mother's bullying. She had tried the wedding dress on before, more than once. She knew it wouldn't take long and that there was still plenty of time. She needed fresh air and she needed time to think.

By the time she reached the top she was breathless and grateful for the iron bench positioned there. She wondered how on earth they had managed to get it up that steep slope.

She sank down on it gratefully and took in the glorious view across the channel to Guernsey. It was a blissfully sunny and peaceful summer's day (apart from the pre-nuptial preparation turmoil below) and the boats of varying sizes chugged or sailed their way through the waters of the channel, leaving white foamy trails behind them.

A distant boom came to her across the water. It was the noon-day gun from Guernsey's Castle Cornet, fired ceremoniously every day. She glanced at her wrist watch, an expensive present (one of many) from Guy. The gun was on time, as ever.

She sighed. What the sigh portended she had no idea. Regret? Apprehension? Relief at being away from the hurly burly if only for a few minutes? Or was it guilt? Guilt that she didn't feel excited about her forthcoming wedding as brides were supposed to?

She closed her eyes and thought of Guy. So debonair, quite a catch, very handsome, well-connected and obviously deeply in love with her; she had no doubt of it. Yes, there was the age difference. His 32 compared to her 22. It had never bothered her before. She had never even thought about it. Why was it bothering her now?

A noise from behind her suddenly distracted her. She rose hurriedly and turned. A woman stood watching her, hands thrust deeply into the pockets of a long coat, her head covered by a headscarf. Odd attire indeed, Issy couldn't help thinking, for such a warm day. That the woman was petite and pretty there was no doubt; a little older than Isobel perhaps.

"Hello," she said hesitantly.

"Good afternoon," the other replied. Issy detected a trace of a foreign accent there.

"The island is very busy today," she continued in what Issy thought might be a German accent. "There is to be a wedding."

"I know," Issy said, "All the turmoil, it's my fault. I'm the bride."

The other woman nodded.

"I wondered. I thought you must be."

"Is it that obvious?" Issy said. She was waiting for the admonition. Why aren't you getting ready? What are you doing wandering about up here? Surely there are so many things a bride should be doing. None came. The woman just looked at her quizzically, a slight smile playing about her lips.

"You look troubled," she said, "Something is on your mind."

It was most definitely a statement and not a question and rather a perceptive one, Issy thought. She did indeed have something on her mind. She had a lot on her mind in fact. She was thinking about her future happiness. And suddenly, she wanted to let it all out.

Why she should suddenly break down and weep in front of a total stranger she didn't know, but that was exactly what she did. The tears started and she began to cry unashamedly.

"Hey. Hey." The stranger was by her side, an arm around

her waist, the other one holding her hand. She felt herself being led back towards the bench.

"Come," the stranger said, "Sit here awhile."

"I'm sorry," Issy managed to say, "I feel so stupid."

"No, no, no, not stupid," the woman re-assured her, "Sometimes it helps to let go."

They sat down, side by side, on the bench. As Issy's crying subsided, the other person sat, holding her hands, looking on sympathetically but totally undemanding. Issy looked at her properly for the first time, noticing that she was older than she had first taken her for.

Although slight of frame, which made her look very girlish, her pale grey eyes contained a wealth of wisdom that tended to make her appear ageless. And Issy could feel strength in her hands, even though her own hands were being held with a gentle tenderness.

"You're not a wedding guest?" Issy asked anxiously, "You're not a friend of my future husband's family, or acquaintances?"

The other shook her head.

"Just re-visiting the island," she explained, "I once lived here. In the distant past."

"I'm from Guernsey; I'm Issy. Isobel Ponsonby-Sloane. Stupid double-barrelled name. A result of my mother's two marriages." She couldn't keep the bitterness out of her voice.

"It is nice to meet you, Isobel Ponsonby-Sloane," the other said, "It might interest you to know that I was also married on Herm."

Issy was indeed interested.

"Really? Did you have the misfortune to have that ridiculous-wedding planner my mother has hired? Hilary Turnbull?"

Her companion smiled. It was a sad wistful smile.

"My wedding was rather a long time ago. I don't think wedding-planners as such existed then. But look. Let's talk about you. Tell me why you are so sad on your wedding day".

If anybody else had asked her that, Issy felt she would have screamed in rage. But somehow, at the top of this walk, in the peace and quiet, with all the crazy world lying well below her, she felt calm and unperturbed. This strange woman's age was difficult to place. Her sincere deep grey eyes and slight accent filled Issy with a sense that she could tell her everything, say anything to her.

"My intended is a lovely man," Issy said, "And I know he loves me. He is a good man. The trouble is…"

She stopped speaking and stared across the Channel. The other waited for a few moments and then prompted her gently. "Yes?"

"Well, he comes from a very well-appointed family on Guernsey, and my mother…"

"Approves the wedding because of the connections she will gain."

"Exactly. You understand. She's just like Mrs Bennett in the book 'Pride and Prejudice'. She doesn't really care for my happiness. I'm sure of it."

"I do not know this book of which you speak. But I can understand your concern. Your mother might see an advantage in you marrying this man, what is his name?"

"Guy Le Prevost."

"Even if she sees your marriage as a good thing, it does not mean that she does not mean for your happiness." She sighed and a look of reflectiveness came over her face. "My husband was a lot younger than me. But I did not care. Because I loved him."

She gripped Issy's hands tightly, looking directly into Issy's eyes. "I loved him you see, so nothing else mattered. Nothing."

Issy stared back into her eyes, unable to break the gaze.

"Listen Isobel Ponsonby-Sloane. Such funny names you Westerners have. Here is the most important question. Do you love this man…this Guy Le Prevost?"

Being faced with the question so directly, Issy was startled, and almost indignant that someone should have asked it.

"Of course I love him. I love him very much. He is ten years older than me, but…"

"Only ten years?" It was said in a gently mocking but kindly fashion.

Issy caught the twinkle in her eye and couldn't help laughing.

"Why marry a young man of your own age who is possibly immature and does not know his way in the world, when you can marry one who is already successful? It is not your mother who is marrying this man. It is you. You tell me you love him and I can see in your eyes that you do. What else is there, Isobel?"

Issy's heart was welling up, as were her eyes. She thought of the wonderful times she and Guy had already had together already and of all the wonderful times they had to come. She let the other's hands go and reached out and took her in her arms to give her a big hug. She was surprised at how slight and fragile she felt in her arms.

"Thank you," she said, "Thank you so much. You've made it all alright again. I'm so glad I met you."

"And now my girl," the other said briskly, "It's time you got back. Everybody down there is expecting a wedding. Don't disappoint them. You are the most important person, the chief player, the principal girl. But above all, the man you love will be waiting for you."

They hugged again and then began their descent down the steep walk.

Issy kept her arm around her new-found friend; as they got closer to the bottom, she felt that her companion was getting frailer with each step. It was almost as if Issy was supporting her completely by the time they got back to the hotel gardens. As if she wasn't there at all.

"You didn't tell me your name," Issy said, "I shall never forget you."

The small frail figure almost seemed to fade away as she moved across the lawn.

"Lulu," she said, "Lulu Blucher."

In spite of the warm day, Issy felt a little chill breeze embrace her momentarily. She wondered if Lulu had felt it too. But Lulu had gone. There was no sign of her. Issy was not certain exactly where she went or at what point she disappeared. She wanted to thank her again. She knew her destiny now. She loved Guy. She was going to marry Guy. And it was thanks to a chance meeting with a lady called Lulu at the top of Princess Radziwell's walk that had brought her to this realization. And she wanted to express those thanks. But it was too late.

Issy hurried back towards the hotel.

~

Hilary Turnbull gave a sigh that sounded like a seal cow coughing. She said:

"It's alright Phoebe. She's back. She's coming towards you. Can you see her? You can? Thank heavens for that. Now for goodness sake, get her back into that hotel room and changed into that trousseau. Who was that funny little woman with her? What do you mean Phoebe, there was no-one with her? She was arm in arm with a woman, a little woman. She seemed to be holding her up. You couldn't see anyone? Well it must be my eyesight then. Obviously. The other woman certainly seems to have disappeared now. But the bride was waving someone goodbye. Oh, never mind. Have you got her, Phoebe? Are you escorting her back? Yes, I can see you are. Thank heavens. Now you make sure everything is all right at your end. I'll check everybody else. I've got a feeling everything is going to be alright now. Yes! I've got a feeling this is going to be Hilary Turnbull's Wedding of the Year!"

~

It was not until much later that Issy put two and two together.

Louise (Lulu) was married to Lothair, the son of Prince Blucher, the tenant of the island. But how could she have been here on Herm now? On Issy's own wedding day?

The answer was not too hard to fathom once you remembered the story. Lothair had been much younger than his bride. He had built the walk for her, Princess Lulu Radziwell, as she became. They were very much in love. But the whole family was forced to leave the island at the onset of the First World War. Because they were German.

Princess Radziwell had never wanted to leave Herm Island. So, she had come back. She had returned to the walk built for her, bearing her name, by the man she loved.

Or had she come back? Maybe Princess Radziwell had never ever really left her own private walk at all. Maybe she is still there. Waiting to talk to the unsuspecting hotel guest who has taken the trouble to climb up there.

~

WHERE SEAGULLS DARE

During the writing of the tales, a friend of mine on Guernsey asked me if I had included a tale set on Herm during the German Occupation of World War II. At the time, I hadn't, but of course once the seed is sown, it begins to nourish and grow. Enter Private Owen Jenkins, the only soldier sent to Herm to 'protect' its two residents. I hope you like the end of this tale. I am rather pleased with it. The story is set at two of the highest points on Herm Island, Monku and the Grand Monceau, both approachable by accessible paths from the Spine Road.

"There's only a couple of residents on Herm Island right now. A retired brigadier and his granddaughter. He's asked for protection and he's an important man."

The officer paused and studied the young private standing at ease in front of him.

"Jenkins. We don't believe for a moment that the Bosch are going to invade Herm."

"Right glad I am to hear it, Sir."

"SPEAK WHEN YOU'RE SPOKEN TO, LAD!" barked the sergeant, standing on his right, his cap pulled so low that there was just a nose protruding between it and his moustache.

"Sarge!" yelled Private Owen Jenkins, snapping to attention.

"Er…at ease Jenkins." The officer made a twirling motion with his fingers. "So, I want you to understand that you are a token presence only. To satisfy the populace, so to speak. Even though there are only two of them. Obviously, if we thought the Gerries were really going to invade, we'd put on a damn sight bigger show. You understand?"

"Sah!" Jenkins replied.

"You'll be dropped at Herm Harbour by boat at twenty-two hundred hours. You will make contact with Brigadier Mortimer-Pryke in the morning. You will radio your report to Guernsey-base at 18:30 every evening. You will have a map of the island, a compass, field-glasses, flashlight, two small short-wave radios, one of which you will give to the Brigadier so you can remain in contact with him, your rifle, a pistol, camping equipment and provisions. Is there anything else you think you'll need?"

"Money for an ice-cream, sir?"

Jenkins felt the sergeant bristling at his side, so he said:

"Just joking sir. Right partial to a drop of ice-cream I am."

"Yes well…" said the officer forcing a laugh and turning it into a cough, "My advice to you Jenkins is…enjoy your sojourn. It's not every member of the British Army who gets to spend his war on an almost deserted island. It's 1940. Play your cards right and you'll still find yourself there in 1941. Don't worry. If the war ends, we won't forget you."

Jenkins was thinking, "I could be in Italy, or North Africa. Or France. What on earth am I going to do on a tiny boring island for a year?"

If truth be told, the place where Private Owen Jenkins really wanted to be was back in the Welsh Valleys wandering through the hills with Rhiannon, his girl.

Private Owen Jenkins made his camp in a field at the top of the island, between Monku and Le Manoir, where he knew the Brigadier lived with his granddaughter. He set up his tent as comfortably as space would allow, his radio by his sleeping bag, his gun on the other side and a photograph of Rhiannon taped above him.

He didn't sleep well. There were seagulls and other birds caterwauling all night, and the sound of the waves did not lull him into the kind of sleep he craved. How was he going to survive this lonely island with just the birds for company? And how long was he expected to stay here? The officer said he might be here for a year. It was a year too long. Could he survive the loneliness? He doubted it.

Tomorrow he would visit the Brigadier. At least there was some human contact.

~

Owen was standing outside Le Manoir, a large mansion house at the top of the island, ten minutes' walk from his 'base'. He gave the bell-pull a hearty tug. Apart from the metallic sound of iron scraping against iron, there was no sound for a moment. Then from inside the house, came the raucous jangling sound of a military march played on a carillon of bells.

Owen Jenkins was startled silly. If that sound didn't repel any German invader of Herm, nothing would. After a minute or two, he heard the sound of bolts being drawn inside the door. Obviously, the Brigadier intended to keep himself secure.

The door slowly opened to reveal the face of a girl. In her late teens Owen guessed, blonde and possessed of a good figure, pretty face and generous lips. Her most striking features were her eyes; Owen could only describe them as 'smouldering'. The granddaughter, no doubt.

"My prayers have been answered," she said huskily, opening the door fully. She was a stunner and no mistake.

Immediately, Owen was filled with feelings of guilt and shame, as a picture of fresh-faced rosy-cheeked Rhiannon came into his mind.

He came to attention and announced himself in his best military manner.

"Private Jenkins, Herm detail, at your service ma'am." He relaxed slightly. "May I please speak with Brigadier Mortimer-Pryke?"

She ran her forefinger down the front of his tunic.

"They've sent me my own personal English soldier," she said, her eyes boring into his, "I've got you all to myself."

"I'm Welsh actually look you," Owen told her. "Now. The Brigadier ma'am. If you would be so kind."

Owen sprang to attention again.

"Welsh is even better," she said, her eyes boring into his. "All that wild Celtic blood."

Owen coughed politely.

"The Brigadier?" he repeated.

"My Grandpa," she said sullenly, "You'd better come in. But we could get better acquainted first, if you like."

She took her finger from off his tunic and placed it in her mouth.

Owen side-stepped her into the hall. He had no time for this. As quick as a lightning-flash, she was in front of him again, tracing her wet finger across his webbing.

"At least let me show you round the island," she pouted, "You'll see all the sights. I'm sure you'd find them... stimulating."

She giggled and thrust her face up towards him, her lips wet and her eyes on fire.

"VERONICA!" A voice thundered across the hall.

The Brigadier was every inch that of a military man. Tall, well-structured, fit, greying only slightly. A severe expression now beset his distinguished face. He marched towards them.

"Veronica! Leave us."

"But Grandpa…"

"Leave us. Go and do a jig-saw puzzle or something."

Veronica sidled towards a door, her thumb in her mouth. As she left, she cast a look back at Owen that promised much more than he could ever accept.

"Come into the study," the Brigadier ordered. "You can give me your name, rank, number. We all need to do our part. We need to discuss strategy."

And so they did. Owen gave Brigadier Mortimer-Pryke the spare radio and briefed him on his role and his orders. The Brigadier seemed satisfied with the arrangements, but as he was showing Owen out, he said:

"Don't think you can come over here, Private Jenkins and have your wicked way with my Veronica. You can keep your nylon stockings and chocolate bars for the girls in St Peter Port. We'll have none of your shenanigans on Herm Island, thank you very much."

Owen didn't dignify the caution with a response. Instead, he replied:

"You have the short-wave radio, Brigadier, for use in emergencies. I am camped between Monku and here. In the event of a German presence on Herm Island, we will use coded messages. Here is a code book. This mustn't fall into enemy hands. And I can assure you, I have brought neither nylon stockings nor chocolate with me. No chewing gum either. Good day Sir."

The nerve of the man. Owen was strict chapel and had his gorgeous Rhiannon back home; he had no interest in the Brigadier's granddaughter whatsoever.

As he left the house, he noticed a pair of eyes watching

him covetously from behind a gap in a door.

⁓

The day passed uneventfully. Owen spent much of the time dozing on the hillside, the Herm sun hot for the time of year. He dreamed of Rhiannon. At one point as his face was close to hers, it changed. It was Veronica whose face he saw, her flame-crazed eyes and moist lips just inches from his own.

With a shocked gasp, he was awake, relieved to find himself alone.

His radio began to buzz. A call was coming through.

"Jenkins? Mortimer-Pryke here? Have you heard the news? The British are leaving Guernsey. They're demilitarizing the island."

"What?"

"I've just heard it on the wireless. The Home Service."

Owen sprang to his feet, grabbed his binoculars and jammed them to his eyes. Sure enough, there seemed to be some movement from out of the harbour at St. Peter Port.

"They can't do that," he murmured to himself, "They can't go without me."

⁓

At six-twenty-five, he prepared himself for his call through to Guernsey-Base. He set up and turned on his radio. Quickly he tuned in to the frequency he had been given for contact.

"Jenkins to Guernsey-Base. Are you receiving me? Over." He flicked the switch to 'Receive'. Nothing. Just a crackle of interference, but very loud.

"This is Private Jenkins, Herm detail, calling Guernsey-Base. Are you receiving me? Over."

He waited. He moved the dial away from the assigned frequency and back again. Still nothing except that infuriating crackling.

He moved the dial back and forth. Nothing. He turned it again, a little more frantically.

"Private Jenkins?" came a sultry female voice over the radio.

Veronica.

"Can you hear me, soldier?"

"Receiving you loud and clear, Miss," he said in his most military voice.

"Can't you get the news on your radio?" she said, "The evacuation has begun."

"The what?"

"Evacuation. They're taking all the Guernsey children to England. Seems like the Germans might be invading the Channel Islands after all."

Owen tried to speak, but couldn't.

"That's the bad news. The good news is, they're leaving you here, soldier boy. Got to go now. Granddad's coming..."

There was a click and silence. Then another click, and the voice added:

"I'm coming to get you soldier boy, never mind the Germans."

Owen shuddered and clicked off the radio.

～

Two days later, Owen was startled by the sound of distant aircraft. He looked towards St. Peter Port to find all hell had been let loose.

German aircraft, recognizable from their Luftwaffe markings, were flying over Guernsey and dropping bombs on the harbour. Owen stood there open-mouthed, not believing what he was seeing. His only thought was for the safety of the poor civilians, now his own regiment had gone. Thank God they had evacuated the children.

Later he contacted the Brigadier by radio. He had no intention of calling on the man in person. He had no wish to bring about happenings from the Herm Harpy.

"Lorry-loads of tomatoes," the Brigadier snorted, "That's all the blighters got. Tomatoes." His tone changed. "Sadly though, there were some casualties."

~

Every day, Owen tried to contact Guernsey-base on his radio. Everyday, he met with failure. But two days after the bombing raid, he managed to pick up the BBC. It was the BBC Home Service. From London. It felt good to hear that voice. With his Welsh brogue inherited from the valleys, Owen usually scorned at the BBC English way of speaking. But not today. Today, it was the sweetest sound that ever fell upon his ears.

Until he heard what it had to say.

"This is the BBC Home Service. Here is the News and this is Alvar Lidell reading it. We are receiving reports that the Channel Islands have been invaded by German forces. A broadcast from Berlin claims that the island of Guernsey is now under German occupation."

If someone had kicked Private Owen Jenkins in the chest, it could not have felt more of a body blow than this.

What to do? What next? He couldn't return to Guernsey. He'd be taken prisoner for sure. Was his only alternative to stay here? Fulfil his duty and protect the two residents, the Brigadier and his hormone-infused granddaughter? What else could he do? Except try to reach his own side with coded messages? But they had left the Channel Islands. For good, it seemed.

A thought struck him. What if the Germans sent a detail over here? At least he was in a place with a good vantage point over to Guernsey. Unless they came under cover of darkness.

One thing he was certain of. If he had to choose between facing the Nazis and Veronica, he knew who he would choose. And it wasn't Veronica.

~

By 23:00 hours, there had been no developments. The Bosch wouldn't send anybody over to Herm tonight would they? Would they? Improbable.

He shone his torch on the picture of Rhiannon, blew her a kiss, said a prayer; that he would return to the valleys as soon as the Allies had won the war, marry Rhiannon and settle down in the valleys to bring forth kids – loads of them. He clicked off his torch and was asleep in minutes.

At about four in the morning, he was woken by scuffling sounds outside his tent.

Swiftly, he was out of his sleeping bag, crouched, rifle in hand. He listened. Hard. There was definitely somebody out there, snooping around. Had the Germans arrived?

Whoever it was, they were creeping up on him slowly and surely. The sound of footsteps crackling on the bracken outside was unmistakeable. Owen held his breath, ready to shoot whoever stuck their head through his tent flap.

He hadn't even got his boots on. How could he face the enemy without them?

His nemesis was right outside the tent. He felt it. He had been holding his breath for so long he felt dizzy, but his heart was hammering so much, he felt his assailant might hear it. Fingers were now feeling for the tent opening.

He cocked his rifle and aimed it.

"Hello soldier!" A female voice.

Veronica! This time, in person.

"What the hell are you playing at girl?" he said. "I could have shot you."

"Never mind soldier, you didn't. But you can show me your weapon if you like."

She was in the tent and on him faster than any Fritz, Otto or Hans would have been.

She came at him like a deranged dervish, clawing at him, gasping with sensuality. Anybody outside the tent might have mistaken the machinations inside for passion. Far from it. The passion was one-sided, and the other side was Owen fighting off Veronica's fevered noisy attentions, whose urgent urges were uninhibited but unwanted.

Just as Owen was losing his first battle of the war, his radio crackled into life.

"Jenkins! Private JENKINS! Mortimer-Pryke here. They're on the way over. The enemy. The Germans, Jenkins. The BOSCH are on their way."

~

Owen pushed the reluctant protesting Veronica outside and struggled into his boots. He dived out of the tent. She staggered away, grumbling. He thrust his field-glasses to his eyes and trained them on the water.

Sure enough, a German gunboat was on its way in the early morning dawn. The wake of the oncoming boat was the only thing disturbing the water. A Swastika flew high from its mast and ten Nazi soldiers stood at the prow around a sub-machine gun, aimed at Herm Island.

Oh, Rhiannon, Rhiannon, remember me! Respect my memory after the war. You can marry someone else. I want you to be happy, girl. I don't mind as long as you name all your children after me. Even the girls.

He watched as the gunboat reached the harbour. Owen couldn't believe what he was seeing. The Germans were unloading a motor-cycle and sidecar. A motorised division.

One of them jammed a pair of field-glasses to his eyes and did a sweep of the island. Owen ducked, hoping the gorse bushes and rocks would conceal his meagre camp. The soldier's field-glasses stopped at one point and Owen watched him freeze. He had seen something.

He searched that direction with his own field glasses. It was Veronica the soldier had seen. She was pacing across a field towards the spine road to get home. The soldier relaxed and appeared to make a joke of it with one of his companions.

He left the boat and kick-started the motor-bike. Owen heard it roar across the quiet island. A few gulls raised a hue and cry in protest.

The German army, in the shape of one man was now mobilized on Herm Island.

~

It didn't take Owen long to find out what the German had in the side-car. Within half an hour of being on the island, he had set up camp at the top of the Grand Monceau high above Shell Beach and positioned land mines on the approach from the spine road.

He then set off for Le Manoir. He knew which direction to take, stepping warily through his own minefield. He had watched Veronica through field glasses as she made her way home.

Owen dived into his tent, switched on the radio and called the Brigadier.

"DISHEVELLED!" the Brigadier shouted at him. "My granddaughter came home this morning dishevelled after returning from your amorous advances. I warned you…"

"LISTEN!" Owen shouted as loud as he dared into the radio. "I didn't touch her mind. She threw herself at me. You ought to keep her on a lead, look you."

"HOW DARE YOU?"

"Brigadier. There's something far more pressing. Fritz is on his way to you. Hide the radio, keep it turned on. Then I can hear everything that occurs."

"Roger!" came the reply. Then the jangling military march that was the Brigadier's doorbell almost deafened him as it blasted from the radio through his headphones.

～

"I have to inform you that I am now ze commandant of zis island and all its inhabitants are under German command."

"I'm sure the seagulls and rabbits won't notice," the Brigadier muttered.

"Ja." Owen heard the German chuckling. "You Britishers and your sense of humour. To show zere is no hard feelings, I have brought you a bottle of ze best German Schnapps. And before I leave, I would consider it an honour if you would join me in a glass."

Damn! The conniving kraut had brought the Brigadier a present. Why didn't his commanding officer think of that? Why didn't he himself think of that? A nice pot of Welsh Cawl or a tin of laver bread would not have gone amiss.

He heard the Brigadier mumbling his thanks and leaving the room to fetch two glasses.

"Hello soldier," came a sexy voice over the radio. "How nice of the Fuehrer to send me you, and to have you all to myself."

Owen closed his eyes in despair. Did the girl have no shame?

He could visualise her, tracing her wet finger over the front of the German's uniform.

～

It was midnight when Owen's radio crackled back into life. He fumbled with the controls and eventually managed to utter a greeting to the Brigadier.

"Jenkins?" came the Brigadier's voice, "Is Veronica with you?"

"Assuredly not Brigadier," Owen replied.

"Are you sure?"

Owen turned over and shone the beam of his torch around the tent.

"I am absolutely sure, Brigadier."

There was an audible sigh over the radio receiver. "Then she's gone off with the damned Bosch." He sighed audibly. "Help me get her back Private Jenkins. Before her honour is besmirched."

It might be too late for that boyo, Owen thought, then said:

"But if I show my hand, my cover is blown."

"Then kill the blighter."

"If he doesn't report back, there'll be a whole flamin' German battalion over here."

"Please help me Jenkins. She's all I've got in the world."

The Brigadier sounded so woe-begone, Owen's heart went out to him. Would he think twice if it was Rhiannon in danger? Of course he wouldn't.

"So be it. Tell me what you want me to do, Brigadier."

"Plainly, a rescue operation is called for. I'll meet you on the spine road in ten minutes."

"But Brigadier," Owen protested, "He's mined the whole slope up to the top. Trying to reach him that way is to be blown to smithereens."

"Then you'll have to climb the cliff from Shell Beach. Have you got climbing gear?"

"Well as it happens, no, I've not!"

"Never mind. You can do it. I'll meet you on Shell Beach in fifteen minutes."

"But Brigadier..."

The radio had gone silent.

~

The sea off Shell Beach was bathed in moonlight. It was just the right kind of night to rescue an over-endowed girl from the clutches of a German soldier, Owen didn't think.

He found the Brigadier at the base of the cliff, wearing a trench-coat and a woolly hat.

He was pacing backwards and forwards, his hands thrust deep in his pockets.

"Like I said, I've got absolutely no climbing equipment," Owen protested, "No ropes, crampons, cleats or such-like."

"Relax," the Brigadier told him, "It's an easy climb. There's plenty of scrub to hold on. And it's not very steep."

"Steep enough mind!" Owen protested, looking up at the forbidding cliff.

"And when I've got Veronica, how do I get her down?" Owen demanded.

"She's been scrambling up and down these hills since she was five. Put her over the edge and she'll get down. She's got the thighs of a mountain goat."

Tempted to comment, Owen thought better of it.

~

By the time he'd reached the top, his fingers were cut and bleeding (he had stupidly forgotten his gloves), his back and his legs were aching and he was wondering what the hell he was going to find when he reached the German camp.

Owen peered over the top of the edge of the cliff.

From inside Fritz's tent, he could make out that there was a lamp burning. Other than that, it appeared to be empty.

It was. Fritz appeared at the top of the path from the spine road, carefully stepping his way through the minefield, shining his torch in front of him.

Where was Veronica? Clearly Fritz hadn't abducted her; she wasn't with him.

Then Owen spotted her. She was trailing Fritz, walking in his footsteps close behind him. What in hell's name did she think she was doing?

But Owen knew only too well what she was doing; she was stalking the German back to his tent. Didn't she know she was walking through a minefield? No, she didn't. Owen had told the Brigadier about them after she had gone missing. How could she?

There was every chance she would be blown to pieces if she so much as stepped away from the route Fritz was taking.

What could Owen do? Warning her would immediately reveal himself to the enemy.

But he couldn't let her die. Thinking about the consequences would come later.

"VERONICA! FREEZE! DON'T MOVE!" he called out. "THERE ARE LAND MINES ALL AROUND YOU!"

Veronica stopped and uttered a stifled little cry of fear; enough for Fritz to hear though. He seemed undecided. First, he shone his torch in Owen's direction, but Owen had ducked below the cliff-edge out of sight, hanging on for dear life.

Fritz turned and saw Veronica frozen to the spot, whimpering in terror. He went straight for the girl and effortlessly picked her up in his arms. Veronica's terror turned into pleasure far too quickly he thought. Clearly, she had no allegiance to any particular side in this war.

Owen watched as Fritz carried the girl, cavorting in his arms, to his tent. He opened the flap and threw her inside, then followed her in. It was only a matter of time before Fritz came to look for him, Owen realised. He glanced down and saw the Brigadier staring anxiously up. Owen couldn't go down empty-handed; the Brigadier would be devastated.

Was this the time for a daring rescue attempt? Did he storm the tent brandishing his pistol and demanding the release of the girl? Would Fritz have any hesitation in shooting him? Was he prepared to shoot Fritz? Owen didn't know.

From inside the tent, came the sound of bedlam. Fritz was having problems of his own. Owen could see their silhouettes through the canvas illuminated by the lamp. Veronica was launching her own personal assault on the enemy in her own inimitable way. Judging by Fritz's yells of protest, his surrender wasn't an option.

Now was the time.

Owen levered himself over the top of the cliff onto the grassy surface of the Grand Monceau. Drawing his pistol, he approached the tent, inside which the pitched battle was enacting itself. The moon shone benignly overhead. The lights of enemy-occupied Guernsey twinkled in the distance. The only war drama being played out seemed to be inside a tent on the Grand Monceau on Herm Island.

Suddenly, Fritz catapulted out of the tent. His uniform and hair were unkempt and he was unarmed. Owen stepped forward, his pistol aimed at the German and said:

"Please remain still. I am a British soldier and you are my prisoner."

Fritz didn't remain still. He launched himself at Owen, in a fevered frenzy, clawing at the front of his uniform.

"Gott in Himmel!" he shouted, "You come at ze right time. Get her off me. She has come straight out of a Wagner opera! Zis is one Valkyrie zat is not going to use me for its ride!"

"Stand still!" Owen said sharply, making a jabbing movement with his pistol. Would he use it if he had to? He hoped he wouldn't have to. Trying to keep his voice calm, he said:

"I am to return this girl to her grandfather, who is waiting for her. He is on Shell Beach below. You will not impede this operation, boyo, or I...or I will have to... shoot you..."

The crazed blue eyes of the German searched his own.

"I understand. Do what you have to do! I will not impede your actions," he said, looking mightily relieved as he said it.

Gun in hand, Owen strode to the tent opening.

"Veronica girl?" he said sternly, "You come out now, and no messing around, mind."

Veronica came out of the tent with as much dignity as she could muster, bearing in mind her make-up was smudged and her clothes were in disarray. She stared at his gun.

"Are you going to use that on me?" she teased. Then, mimicking a poor Welsh accent, she added: "You have a masterful way about you, boy from the valleys. I'm spoilt for choice now I am. Is this what Mata Hari must have felt like?"

Owen took her by the arm and marched her to the cliff top. If Fritz had wanted to take command of the situation, he could have done so there and then. But he was too pre-occupied with re-arranging his uniform.

"Climb down," Owen ordered her, "There's your

granddad. He's waiting look you."

She came at him, grabbed him with both arms and pressed her lips firmly against his, giving him a souvenir, which if he survived the war, he could take back to the valleys (Oh Rhiannon, sorry, but she just came at me. Evasive action was out of the question!)

As Veronica broke away, Owen realised he had dropped his pistol. He saw it skid to the edge and then roll over in slow motion.

Veronica followed. The brigadier was right. She did have the thighs of a mountain goat.

He was about to follow her, when Fritz's voice stopped him in his tracks.

"Now you are my prisoner, Britisher," he said, his gun firmly trained on Owen. "You are unarmed and I have, how you say, ze upper hand."

He motioned his gun for Owen to enter the tent. Cursing Veronica's advances and his own stupidity, he did as he was told.

Fritz approached him, sheathing his gun into his holster. He burst out laughing and offered Owen his hand.

"Dieter," he announced, "Dieter Werner."

"Owen Jenkins." Owen grasped his hand.

"To celebrate my rescue from the sexy junges Mädchen, I owe you a drink. Schnapps?"

Chapel and abstinence in the valleys seemed a millennium away.

"Don't mind if I do Dieter boyo."

"Gut! And we sing. We drink and we sing. Maybe tomorrow, we resume the war. After ze hangover ist gone? What do you say Owen, mein freund?"

"Sounds lush to me," Owen replied.

❧

THE CASE OF THE
POISONED PINOT

Wine tasting weekends in the White House Hotel are a regular feature of the Herm Island tariff and therefore I had to have a story set during one of them. There was also once a murder mystery weekend in the hotel, which I happened to be on the island for, so I decided to combine the two. However, I took it a stage further and made the murder real. Add a few larger-than-life characters including a very silly sleuth, season with a force 9 gale so the island becomes a microcosm, and you have the longest story in the book. Fitting, I thought therefore, that it should be the final tale.

"This wine is awful. In fact, it's terrible. No, worse, it's disgusting."

The penetrating voice of the big Californian boomed across the lounge at a volume of decibels not normally associated with a human voice, and he wasn't even shouting.

Lucinda Borger, an eminent wine-grower from Sittingbourne in Kent, England, (whose wine it was being criticized) cringed, along with everybody else.

"The truth of the matter is," Cephas B. Strawboulder continued, "You Brits can't hope to make a decent wine. You don't have the sunshine to grow an acceptable grape."

It was the annual wine-tasting weekend on Herm Island at the White House Hotel. Cephas B. Strawboulder had come all the way from California to bless the company with his presence and his wines. Within minutes, the assembled company soon learned that Cephas B's presence was more of a curse than a blessing.

Especially Mrs Lucinda Borger, who had attended the event for several years now and whose wines in the past had earned her the warmest compliments from the Guernsey folk making up the majority of the wine-tasting complement.

Now she had come face to face with the boorish Mr Cephas B, whose Californian wines from his own vineyard were the finest in the Western hemisphere, you better believe it, buddy! He wasn't finished with Mrs Borger yet.

"Its nose is tacky, it clings to the glass like syrup, its initial taste is like vitriol and it leaves an after-taste of brackish ditch water."

There was silence in the lounge. Nobody liked to contradict Cephas B, although everybody wanted to. Cephas B was not the sort of man you confronted in public. Yet, several of the wine-tasting guests had been drinking Mrs Borger's wine and found it very palatable indeed.

Lucinda desperately wanted to take on this bombastic bully. Take him on? She wanted to kick him, to claw his eyes out, knee him in the nuts, push a stiletto blade through his rolls of fat, although she doubted if she would find any vital organs.

She fervently wished she could have slipped something potent into his glass. She'd give him tacky. She'd give him vitriol. She'd give him brackish.

Instead she gave him a fatuous comment.

"I don't know your name," she said, "But I doubt if you could tell the difference between a sauvignon and a soubriquet."

Cephas B threw back his head and roared such a laugh that seemed to make the window frames rattle.

"Tonight, my dear lady," he informed her, "Before supper, I will let you taste my Californian Blush. There is a box coming over on the last boat. One of many. I will be delighted to instruct you in the delights of real wine. Not your Brit crap."

Lucinda deigned not to reply this time. She had already given him too much satisfaction with her lack of pithy responses. Doubtless, once in her hotel room, she would think of a dozen cutting, witty remarks she could have thrown at him and floored him with. It was always the way.

"Violet!" Cephas suddenly yelled. Was there no limit to this man's volume in decibels? Clearly not, as the resonating ear-drums of the assembled company testified.

A small pale woman, whom nobody had noticed before, suddenly detached herself from a chair and appeared, as if for the first time.

"This is my wife," Cephas B announced. "Violet. My shrinking violet I like to call her."

Violet was dressed in a pale violet dress. Her hair was collected up in a bun, held together with what looked like two thick knitting needles.

"I could call her Violent Violet," Cephas B remarked, "But that she ain't. Are you honey?"

"Not if you say so dear," Violet acquiesced.

"It's time for our siesta, Violet." Cephas B hoisted his own expansive frame out of the chair. As he got up, it seemed to sigh with relief.

"I shall take a short stroll dear," she told him.

"But our siesta Violet…"

"A short stroll dear…"

"Siesta."

189

"Stroll."

"There you are, you see." Cephas B laughed it off. "Not always so shrinking, but that's about as violent as Violet gets."

He turned to Lucinda.

"Listen lady," he said and for a moment Lucinda thought he sounded like a character out of a *film noir*. "Forget your wine growing in that Great UK of yours. Come to California. I can always find you a job as a bottle-washer."

He guffawed and strode out of the lounge, followed by his shrinking Violet. Lucinda was left fuming, but speechless.

A voice from the corner said in a low voice, "You know there's hemlock on the island?"

They were gone.

~

The last boat, carrying Cephas B's precious consignment of Californian Blush only just arrived. Clearly there was a force 9 brewing with black brooding clouds overhead scudding with an intense velocity across the sky. The sea sounded angry and the wind whined away in all directions on the island.

The Trident crew and the island staff had a tough task unloading and loading.

An assorted bunch of visitors to Herm Island disembarked that evening. Among them were the residual wine-tasters here for the event, whose late arrival had deprived them of the spectacle of the 'wine war' between Cephas B. Strawboulder and Mrs Lucinda Borger from Kent.

Another group of arrivals might have been taken for

a party of Italian holiday-makers. They were over for an evening meal in the Ship and afterwards, accommodation in assorted cottages; they chattered noisily in their mother-tongue and made their way from the harbour, waving their arms about a lot.

Following them ashore, hardly unobtrusively, was a tall thin young man with a hook nose and eager eyes. Hardly unobtrusive because of the way he was dressed.

Deerstalker, cape, leggings, carrying a violin case and a pipe firmly wedged between his teeth.

"Bloody hell, it's Sherlock Holmes," one of the island porters observed.

"Indeed it is, my man," said the character, who was the very epitome of that famous sleuth. "I am here for the Sherlock Holmes Convention. I wonder if you would point me in the right direction."

The porter looked at his mate.

"Sherlock Holmes Convention?" he said, "I don't think that's going on here this weekend, Sir. Do you Ron?"

His co-worker shook his head.

"Nah. I thought as how I heard tell there was one on Sark. But not here."

The young man's face brightened.

"That's right. Sark!" he chimed. Then his face fell. "This isn't Sark, is it?"

"No Sir, I'm afraid not. This is Herm."

"The deuce, Watson." He turned to an imaginary companion. "We've come to the wrong island."

Then he brightened again.

"Oh well, thanks gentlemen. Maybe you could point me in the direction of Sark."

"We can point you in that direction," said the porter who wasn't Ron, "But you won't be getting there tonight."

He indicated the Trident which had pulled well away from the Harbour.

"Jolly good grief Watson," he said, "Flummoxed!"

Then to the men: "Can you call her back?"

"Call her back? In this weather? No chance. Anyway, even if you got back to Guernsey, you won't get a boat to Sark till tomorrow. If then. Depends on this gale abating."

"I take it there's accommodation in one of the hotels here?" Holmes asked.

"They might be able to put you up in *the* hotel. The White House. There's only one. But it is the wine tasting weekend. It'll be pretty full."

"Come along Watson," the singular young gentleman said, "This is one mystery that isn't going to be solved by procrastination."

And 'Sherlock Holmes' strode off, violin case in one hand and travelling bag in the other.

"Who does he keep talking to, Mark?" the one called Ron said, "There's no one with him."

"Well if he's Sherlock Holmes," the one called Mark said, "He obviously thinks he's got Doctor Watson with him."

"Doctor Watson?"

"Yes. Helped him solve all his cases. And wrote all the stories about them."

"Oh, got a bit of screw loose then."

"Possibly not. Just takes himself a bit too seriously."

Angus Dunwoody, aka Sherlock Holmes, was finding it hard to take himself seriously as he suddenly found himself being swept along by the Mediterranean party, who were in fact Sicilian. Although largely speaking Italian, they were using a local dialect which Dunwoody recognised as rural Sicilian, spoken only on Sicily, and

192

indeed, the colloquial language of the famed Mafioso. As a specialist in crime, he had made it his business to study all branches of skulduggery.

"Interesting, Watson," he murmured, as they bore him along at their speed, apparently not realising he was not one of them, so engaged were they in their arm-flapping and intense conversation. "The mob is here. Being on the wrong island might not turn out to be such a bad thing after all."

~

"There you are Mr Dunwoody," said the receptionist, handing him the key. "You're lucky. We had a last-minute cancellation. Room 4. Up the stairs, second room on the right."

"Thank you so much," the young man said, "What time is dinner?"

"Seven until nine," she told him. "But you're welcome to join the wine tasters in the lounge before dining if you wish."

"That sounds an eminently attractive proposal. Come along Watson."

And he strode off up the stairs.

Puzzled, the receptionist said: "Watson?"

Another member of staff said:

"He's Sherlock Holmes. Watson is his side-kick."

"But he was alone."

"Role play," the other whispered, "Apparently, he's supposed to be at a Sherlock Holmes convention on Sark. Maybe his own personal Watson managed to get it right."

In a flash, Dunwoody was back at reception.

"I'm sorry, but you wouldn't happen to know..."

"Mr Dunwoody?" the receptionist enquired politely.

"There isn't a Professor Moriarty staying here this weekend is there?"

The receptionist checked her guest list.

"No sir," she informed him, "At least, not under that name."

"Thank you." He long-legged it up the stairs to his room, dropping his key and retrieving it in a single swoop on the way.

"Professor Moriarty?" the receptionist demanded of her companion.

"Sherlock Holmes' arch-enemy," came the reply, "They had a fight at the Reichenbach falls."

"Oooh. He does take himself, seriously doesn't he?"

∼

Mabel and Doris were from Halifax but had been coming to Herm for years. They had just had their first constitutional sherry of the evening, in the Monk's bar.

They reached the foot of the stairs, just as the 'eminent sleuth' was ascending.

"Ee, look at that Mabel," remarked Doris, "I think that's Sherlock Holmes."

"Oh, does he come here then?"

"Well it's not really him," Doris told her. "But you know what this means, don't you? It's not only the wine-tasting. It looks as if there's a murder mystery weekend as well."

"Oh, what fun," Mabel clapped her hands together. "Maybe we can solve it and win a bottle of sherry."

∼

The wine-tasters were gathered. They were rather a refined well-to-do class of people, if a little wrapped up in their own world of viniculture. But they were certainly polite to each other, even if between gritted teeth when they were discussing the particular merits of a certain wine. But they were a jolly lot who 'got on really well together, don't you know, what?'

There was an especial bond about them before dinner this evening. They were all agreed to a man (and woman) that no boastful, brash, boorish American was going to beat them into any sort of submission. It was all European viniculturists together this evening. Nobody, but nobody was going to say anything even vaguely congratulatory about the Californian wines of Mr Cephas B. Strawboulder.

They were all dressed for dinner and gathered in the lounge, a glass of their preferred vintage held delicately in their fingers. There was an uneasy silence amongst them as they waited for the two people who had not yet come down for the pre-prandial wine tasting.

Mr Cephas B. and Mrs Violet Strawboulder. Once they had arrived, then let battle commence.

Still they stood in silence waiting for the footsteps that would herald the arrival of the arch-enemy. They expected to hear only one set of footsteps because that mouse of a wife was so light on her feet. Cephas on the other hand would be heavy-footed and no-one would ever mistake his approach.

Grimaces and severe looks settled on all faces as footsteps approached the lounge. Cephas B. Strawboulder staggered in, red-faced and puffing with the exertion of carrying a box of his bottles of wine. His mousy wife, Violet, meekly followed him, a look of eternal apology on her face, which she was doubtless always forced to wear, given the over-bearing nature of her spouse and the effect he had upon any assembled company who were forcedly subjected to him.

"Friends!" he announced in a grandiose fashion as if he were surrounded by friends.

In fact, all the pairs of eyes on him were far from friendly. There was hostility in the air, particularly from Mrs Lucinda Borger, the Kentish lady, whose wine he had publicly slated earlier in the day.

"Friends!" he said again, as if to convince himself again that all the folk there were indeed friends. "Cephas B is about to regale you with the greatest wine-tasting experience you will savour this weekend, or indeed, any weekend – my Californian Blush."

Californian or not, there was no way that any sort of blush would ever have adorned Cephas B's face. He was not the blushing type, neither would he ever feel abashed, ashamed or intimidated. Cephas B was the Viscount of Viniculture, the Warlord of Winemaking.

"This, people…" Maybe not sensing much friendship, he had changed his form of address from 'friends' to 'people'. "This is a treat waiting to burst upon your palates, a sensation awaiting your anticipation. I am popping the cork."

With this grand pronouncement, Cephas B proceeded to do just that. But it didn't 'pop' so much as crawl out of the neck of the bottle. Bits of broken cork feathered the air. Cephas B was confounded and turned a different shade of red.

"Folks!" People had now been relegated to folks. "I cain't understand what's happening heah," he proclaimed, "I don't normally get a bum bottle in my bin. But I'm gonna show you that Cephas B's wine is good, however it comes."

He poured a generous portion of the rose-tinted fluid into a glass, held it up to the light and watched the reflections of the chandeliers twinkling in the wine.

He should have sniffed it first; everyone said so afterwards. Then he might have lived.

Not that anyone was overly concerned. Especially Mrs Lucinda Borger from Kent.

There were those who swore afterwards that they had not actually seen Cephas B imbibe any of the wine. Others swore they saw him take a large swallow; yet others would have testified to a small gulp. But they all uttered horrified gasps at what happened next.

Seconds after the wine glass reached his lips, all hell broke loose. First the glass and the bottle went crashing to the floor, yet Cephas B remained standing there, his hands outstretched as if he was still holding them. He could have been performing in a Shakespearean tragedy. The grotesque look on his face was the kingliest of leers.

Then his eyes rolled in an anti-clockwise direction and he began to emit choking, gurgling sounds. His tongue came out and it had taken on a hue as distinctly purple as his face. It was swollen and bulbous.

Then Cephas B. Strawboulder began to shake uncontrollably. Indeed, there were some folk in the assembled company who thought he might fall apart, he was vibrating so violently. The choking sounds had become high-pitched squeaks. Finally, his perambulations brought him crashing to the floor, where he lay twitching and writhing in apparent pain and torment.

Everybody stared down at him aghast, including Violet, his dedicated if down-trodden spouse. Her eyes were moving rapidly in alarm and she looked as if she was trying to stifle a scream. There was a scream but it wasn't Violet. It was a high-pitched whistling screaming noise from Cephas B's lungs just before he died and finally lay still.

"Wow! That must have been some vintage."

It was the only thing that Mrs Lucinda Borger from Kent could think of to say.

Probably her finest *bon mot*.

At that point, there might have been pandemonium and mayhem had it not been for a purposeful if almost falsetto voice taking command of the situation.

"Nobody will move please." Nobody moved. Nobody had seen the self-styled Sherlock Holmes lookalike come into the room. He was now standing just inside the doorway, fully kitted out as the sleuth he purported to be.

"The game's afoot Watson," he cried as he threw himself onto his knees by the side of the dead man.

"It's started." Doris nudged Mabel in the ribs. Mabel, having had more than one pre-prandial sherry than usual, had dozed off.

"What 'as?" Mabel enquired, totally oblivious of the unfolding situation.

"The murder mystery," Doris said. "That big American fella is dead."

"Really?" Mabel said.

"No. Not really," Doris told her. "He's just pretending. Acting. It's a murder mystery weekend. It's started. You missed a lovely death."

"Oh, we'd better have another sherry then," said Mabel.

Mr Angus Dunwoody, alias 'Sherlock Holmes', besides being a revered member of the Arthur Conan Doyle Commemoration Society and Sherlock Holmes impersonator, was also a bit of an amateur sleuth and had in fact assisted the police in his home town of Ballsbury-on-Sea on a number of occasions. It seemed he had taken on the investigation of the Californian wine-producer's death.

He was currently sniffing eagerly at the contents of the bottle that Cephas B had dropped moments before.

"Poisoned!" he declared, "Watson, what do you make of it?"

He held out the bottle to his imaginary companion.

"Hemlock!" he stated dramatically, "Or my name isn't Sherlock Holmes."

His name wasn't Sherlock Holmes as it happened, but he seemed assured that it was hemlock poisoning that had caused Cephas B's untimely demise.

He leaned over Cephas' body and examined the dead man's face, prised his lips open with his fingers, smelt his breath and examined his teeth.

"Hmmm," he said, "Singularly curious."

Cephas B. Strawboulder lay there, his open mouth in a grimace showing his carefully crafted Californian dentures.

From that moment on, everybody seemed happy to address Angus Dunwoody as Mr Holmes, mainly because most of them didn't know his real name.

"Hemlock does grow on the island," murmured someone in the wine tasting brigade who seemed to know about these things, "But how do you know it's in the wine?"

"Madam," he said, pulling himself up to his full height which was not inconsiderable, "Take a sniff." He proffered the bottle. "The smell of parsnips. Or rather, parsnips gone off. Or even the smell from someone who has been eating parsnips twelve hours before."

He took the bottle back and peered at it whilst shaking it gently.

"Look at the residue at the bottom. The glabrous leaves. And do I detect small pieces of green stem, marked with purple streaks? Yes, definitely *Conium maculatum*, commonly known as poison hemlock."

He fixed his beady gaze on the shocked group of people, some of them in a state of disbelief.

"I shall want to interrogate everybody here," Sherlock said. "Including the staff."

"Oughtn't we to notify the police?" suggested a gentleman with a military moustache that seemed to obscure most of his face.

"Yes, my friend, I agree. Inspector Lestrade ought to be in on this," Sherlock mused, "But I understand from reception that the stretch of water to Guernsey is too perturbed to be crossed. The telephones are down as is the Internet. Now, I wish to begin my investigations."

If he was wondering who he should start with, he needn't have worried. One of the chambermaids, pale-faced and frightened, was issued in by the hotel manager. She was carrying a kettle.

"This is Lucy. She has something to report, Mr Holmes," he said, "Something she found in one of the rooms."

"Is there somewhere I can conduct my investigations?" he asked.

"There's a room beyond the Monk's Bar sir, by the exit to the swimming pool. The Garden Room. You're welcome to use that. I'll make sure nobody ventures that far."

"Thank you, most kind, most kind. Come Lucy."

He led the shaking girl into the designated room. She was clearly very frightened.

"Now, what have you to tell me? In precise detail if you would, and leave nothing out."

"Well, sir…" the hapless Lucy began, "I went into this bedroom to turn down…"

"Music too loud, was it?" interrupted Holmes.

"Oh no sir, not that sort of turning down. Turning

down the bedclothes. It's a service we offer guests if they want it."

"I see. Pray proceed."

"Well." The girl leaned forward conspiratorially. Suddenly she seemed to enjoy being the centre of attention. "There was a strange smell in the room."

"Did you recognise this smell?"

"Well, sort of sir, it was like…well…gone-off parsnips."

"Ha!" shouted Holmes in triumph. "What did I tell you Watson?"

The girl looked around, puzzled. Finding no-one else in the room, she continued with her story.

"Then I saw the kettle."

"Kettle?"

"Yes, this one. Lying on its side it was. And the carpet was all wet. And it was that what was causing the smell. So, I picked the kettle up…"

"Was it still warm? Had it been boiled?"

"Oh yes sir. Still steaming. But it was what was inside that turned my stomach. Well, take a look."

Holmes took the kettle, flipped off the lid and looked inside. The kettle was stuffed with a vegetable or plant. Loads of it. All soggy, like it had indeed been boiled up. And the stems were covered with purple patches. The smell of rotting parsnip was overwhelming.

"A hemlock infusion." Holmes' face took on a dark hooded look and he was nodding his head so hard, it looked as if his deerstalker might fall off. "The plot thickens, Watson."

"If you say so sir, but my name's Lucy."

"Quite so. Good girl for knowing your own name off by heart. I was actually addressing…well, never mind. Thank you, Lucy. That will be all. Oh, one more thing."

"Sir?"

"In which room did you find the kettle?"

"Oh, in room 2 Sir."

"Thank you."

Holmes sat for a moment, pulling on his unlit pipe.

"A very singular case Watson," he said to the empty room, "It has all the hallmarks of that case we solved in Wigan – you remember? 'The Adventure of the Bronze Buttock.' I venture to say we will ascertain the perpetrator of this deed before we sit down to dinner, or my name isn't Sherlock Holmes."

His name still wasn't Sherlock Holmes, but notwithstanding, he seemed positive he would be able to identify the villain…and within the hour.

The door from the Monk's Bar suddenly opened and Holmes was beset by two excited elderly ladies bustling in, looking as if they may have had a sherry or two too many.

"He's very good, isn't he?" said Mabel, then to Holmes, "I say, you're very good!"

"Last time we had that Hercules Poirot," Doris added, "He was good too."

"Complete with his little moustache."

"And a French accent."

"I think you will find, Madam," Holmes informed them, "That *Hercule* Poirot was Belgian."

"Well it's all over that way somewhere isn't it?" Mabel said, "By the way, did you bring your violin?"

"Are you going to give us a recital?" Doris asked. "We love that Hungarian Rhapsody."

Sherlock Holmes, aka Angus Dunwoody strode out of the Garden Room back into the lounge and addressed the assembled company.

"Ladies and gentlemen," he said, "Permit me to enquire,

but who is staying in Room 2?"

There was a pause, during which people shuffled unhappily around. Nobody wanted to be in Room 2 at this precise moment and of course, most of them weren't but one person was and they waited for that person to declare themselves.

A voice from the corner of the lounge said:

"I am in Room 2."

It was none other than that most maligned producer of wine, Mrs Lucinda Borger from Kent.

"So, Watson…" Holmes said to the empty space on his right, "We appear to have our murderess. Step forward Madam."

Lucinda did but there was an air of defiance about her. She looked like a woman about to do battle all over again.

"Alright. It's no secret I hated him. Anyone here will tell you that. They are all witnesses to our altercation this morning. He insulted me. And he insulted my wine. He was a pig. If the truth be known, everybody in this room hated him. Any one of them could have done it. But I assure you, *I* didn't."

"But the kettle full of hemlock was found in your room," Holmes insisted. "Your room is where the fatal infusion was concocted. And as you say, you have a motive. Mr Strawboulder violated your vintage."

"When I left my room to come down for dinner, the kettle was untouched."

"But when Lucy the maid went in to turn down the bed, the kettle was lying on its side, spilling its deadly contents on the carpet. I have but one niggling doubt in my mind that does not make this an open and shut case yet."

"Only one?" someone said.

"Yes. I am not yet clear on how the infusion was

administered to the wine. In which room was Mr Cephas B. Strawboulder staying?"

"Room 3," ventured one of the staff.

"And three follows two does it not? Ergo, the two rooms are adjacent. This case is open and shut after all. It becomes more shut than open by the moment."

"How am I supposed to have got into room 3 without a key?" Mrs Borger demanded. "How would I have had time? How could I have done it? To get in, uncork the bottle, pour some away, add the hemlock, then re-insert the cork and make my escape?"

"Ah so you admit it," Holmes cried triumphantly, "A confession, Watson."

"I admit nothing," Mrs Borger cried, "And anyway, you're not even a real detective. Why are we listening to this man? Shouldn't we wait until the police arrive?"

"Inspector Lestrade will not be attending this crime Madam," Holmes said. "I presume he is on Sark. I imagine he got the correct island for the convention."

"I say you're a very good actress you know," Mabel told Mrs Lucinda Borger. The two ladies from Halifax had followed Holmes into the lounge.

"I beg your pardon? What are you implying?"

"Well, all the evidence points to you, doesn't it?" said Doris, "Motive? Opportunity? You're my first choice. But if you want to throw me off the scent, mine's a sherry."

Mrs Lucinda Borger looked as if she was going into some sort of apoplectic fit, likely to match that of Cephas B's before he so dramatically and tragically shuffled off his mortal coil.

But at that moment, fate delivered another twist.

A sudden agonized scream echoed through the ground floor of the hotel.

One of the waiters from the Ship Restaurant rushed into the lounge, red-faced and steaming.

"There's been another one," he cried. "One of the Italians has snuffed it!"

"Italians?" Sherlock echoed. "You mean Sicilians. Watson? The plot thickens even further. If the game was afoot before, it's two feet now."

He turned harshly to Mrs Lucinda Borger of Kent.

"Do not leave the island. You are still my chief suspect."

The force nine gale outside hit the windows with all the force of an angry ogre.

"I'll try not to slip away in my kayak," Mrs Lucinda Borger said.

In Nano-seconds, Sherlock was at the scene of the new death.

~

If the hotel lounge was in disarray, the Ship restaurant was in chaos.

Sherlock Holmes took in the scene. A sizeable Sicilian assembly were slicing the air with their arms in operatic fashion, babbling at each other, mainly in Italian but with their obscure Sicilian words thrown in, and looking very much like a scene from a 'Godfather' film.

A thin pale woman in a black dress, with a veil to match, stood by the luxurious dining table, her hand to her head which was thrown back in a most dramatic manner. It was her agonised scream that had rung through the hotel. Her large tears were carrying voluminous quantities of makeup down her cheeks.

But centre stage, across that very same table, lay one of the guests in a pose that suggested his last gesture had been posthumous. Quite dead. Clutched in his hand, a wine glass. By that very same hand, a bottle of Cephas B. Strawboulder's Californian Blush.

The weeping Niobe was the grieving widow no doubt.

"Nobody touch anything!" Sherlock Holmes screamed, wrenching the wine glass from the dead man's fingers. He sniffed at the glass with his somewhat protuberant nose. Then he leant over the table and examined the lips and teeth of the second victim.

"Gone-off parsnips!" he proclaimed.

All the Sicilians ceased their squabbling, grabbed their glasses, raised them to their lips and echoed:

"Gone-off parsneeps!" they all cried with Sicilian accents, thinking it was a kind of Herm Island toast to the dead man. The Sicilian widow punctuated their toast with a series of gulping sobs.

"Stop!" screamed Sherlock, fearing that other glasses may contain the hemlock-infused wine.

"Stop!" the Sicilians all cried, but it was too late. They all necked their vino.

Sherlock looked around and breathed a sigh of relief. Nobody else seemed to have imbibed the poisoned wine. He picked up the nearest bottle. The label read 'Sittingbourne Vineyards'.

"The deuce Watson," he declared, "They're all drinking the wine of Mrs Lucinda Borger from Kent."

From the far end of the restaurant, a short fat man with a black curly moustache was making his way towards Sherlock Holmes, aka Angus Dunwoody. He seemed vaguely familiar to Holmes. He offered his hand.

"Monsieur 'Olmes?" he said, " 'Ercule Poirot. At your service. But I 'ave to inform you, that the case of the deceased Sicilian…is mine."

"You jest, Monsieur Poirot," Holmes said, "Are you really

Hercule Poirot, or like me, are you…an impersonator?"

Poirot leaned forward and whispered in a coarse Essex accent:

"Of course I am. Reggie Lampwick from Billericay. Supposed to be at an Agatha Christie convention on Alderney. But I got the wrong bleeding island, didn't I?"

"OOOH LOOK!" came an unmistakeable Halifax accent, "Hercules is here as well. Monsewer Porriot. That's got to be worth another sherry."

～

Holmes had decided that there was no room for two famous detectives investigating the case. He dragged Reggie Lampwick from Billericay aside, ripped off his moustache and deposited it in a conveniently adjacent plant-pot.

"Ow!" the denuded ex-Belgian detective yelled, "That hurt. What did you do that for?"

"Sorry my friend, but I was here first therefore I take priority."

"My lip's sore," complained Reggie.

"I have some soothing embrocation amongst my accoutrements which I will fetch for you on one condition," Holmes told him.

"And what's that?" said Reggie, furiously rubbing the space between his nose and his lip.

"That for the duration of this case you agree to become my Dr. Watson."

"I don't like it Squire," the aggrieved Reggie said, "And I don't like you much…"

"How's the space above your lip?"

"Alright, you win! Get me the soothing embrocation."

～

Mabel and Doris, who had been eavesdropping around the other side of the plant, were delighted.

"I'm so glad he's got his Watson now," Mabel said, "It's so much better than talking to thin air and calling it Dr. Watson."

"More realistic," added Doris.

～

The investigation into the second murder began. First to be interviewed was the grieving widow.

"Madam, I commiserate with you on your loss. But I must ask you please, what is…er…was…the name of your husband?"

"Giulio Corionetto. From Sicily." She seemed to spit out the last phrase with some venom.

"Quite so. Giulio Corionetto from Sicily. And do you have any other relatives here with you on this occasion?"

"No. Just one Corionetto! From Sicily!"

"Do you have any reason to suspect anyone of wanting to harm your husband?"

"I didn't. But I do now." She withdrew a crumpled tear-stained card from her black lace sleeve and handed it over.

Holmes took it, uncrumpled it and read the words it bore:

"Signor Corionetto, please accept this very special gift of this bottle of Californian Blush from an unknown admirer."

"A lethal gift," Watson observed, "A murderous present. A fatal token."

"A leprous distilment indeed," mused Holmes, then he turned again to the Widow Corionetto.

"Madam, in what line of business was your late husband

engaged?"

"I don't see what this can possibly have to do with poor Giulio's murder. If you must know, he was in the wine trade."

Holmes' brow clouded over as suddenly as an October Herm sky. Then it cleared just as suddenly.

"Quite so, Madam. That will be all for now. Do not leave the island."

Thunder rumbled overhead and rain hit the windows.

As the Widow Corionetto turned to leave, Violet Strawboulder appeared in the doorway. Both women stopped and glared at each other venomously for a second.

Static electricity seemed to build up between them, the air heavily charged with it.

"Harridan!" hissed the Strawboulder.

"Harpy!" mouthed the Corionetto.

"Hag!"

"Hellion!"

A second later, the two female bodies became one as with howls of rage, they sprang at each other and engaged in the most violent of unarmed combat that Holmes had ever witnessed in his life. They became a hissing writhing ferment of entangled black nylon and flailing fingernails, going for each other's eyes like furies on a field trip.

"Not such a Shrinking Violet now," Holmes observed looking at the Strawboulder woman with her pale arm around the neck of the Widow Corionetto, trying to strangle her. Both arm and neck were bulging with outstanding purple-blue veins. "More like a Poison Ivy."

Some of the wine-tasting guests and Sicilians had piled into the Garden Room. They began to take sides, cheer their favourite combatant on; some were even laying odds and placing wagers.

Eventually, members of the hotel staff managed to pull the two women apart, much to the disappointment of the spectators. Grumbling at being deprived of their entertainment, they shuffled away.

Bedraggled, their clothes in disarray, the two women stood breathing heavily, with clawed faces, glaring at each other. Then, almost in perfect unison, they pointed accusing fingers at each other and cried:

"SHE KILLED MY HUSBAND!"

～

"Flamin' heck," Mabel said to Doris, "They're good actors, aren't they? They make it look so real."

"Not 'alf," Doris replied, "They must get through gallons of that fake stage blood."

～

"So, Watson, the intrigue seems to centre upon the wine business," Holmes postulated, "We have two producers of wine and one importer. What do you make of it? All the clues are there. Right in front of your eyes. I just wish I knew what they pointed to."

"If I was still Hercule Poirot, I might be able to make some deductions. But you have reduced me to the role of Watson, and therefore, I am not able."

"Does it not strike you as improbable that both Cephas B. Strawboulder and Giulio Corionetto happen to be on this small island at the same time? At a wine-tasting event, no less?"

"And Mrs Borger?"

"…has been coming here for years."

"She has motive."

Holmes screwed his eyes up in thought.

"Indeed she does. For the first murder. But why should she also do away with Giulio? Especially as the Corionetto party seemed to have invested in her wine to no small degree. Bottles labelled 'Sittingbourne Vineyards' populated the table. They were all drinking it. Except of course, for the poor host of the party himself, who merely thought he was partaking of an anonymous gift."

"Then it's Violet. Strawboulder's wife," concluded Watson, "Killed hubby because he was a bully and then sent the poisoned wine to the Sicilian."

"With what motive?"

"O.K. I've got it. Giulio's wife killed Strawboulder first. Because he was a rival to her husband. Then Violet, in revenge, killed the Sicilian. That would explain the scrap between the two women."

"So, Giulio cheerfully drank the poisoned wine that his wife had killed Strawboulder with?"

"I hadn't thought of that."

"Besides, how could Giulio have got access to Strawboulder's Californian Blush in order to poison it?"

"Hadn't thought of that either." Watson wrung his hands together in anguish.

"I assure you, Watson, that the perpetrator of both crimes is the same man…or woman."

"Oh Holmes, if you'd only let me be Poirot again. I could think so much more clearly."

"Out of the question. We must work together, not against each other."

"I hate you!" Watson said grumpily.

"There is something you can do for me," Holmes said suddenly, "A piece of information which may help everything fall into place. Go to reception. Find out who booked to come to Herm first. Corionetto or

Strawboulder?"

"Is that important?"

"It is of the utmost urgency."

Still bewailing his woe at being prevented from portraying Poirot, Dr. Watson, aka Reggie Lampwick of Billericay, strode off. At the door, he turned.

"If I do this, can I have some more of the soothing embrocation?"

"Of course," Holmes assured him.

Holmes caught up with Mrs Borger as she was making her way up the stairs to her room.

"May I have a moment of your time, Mrs Borger?" he said.

"Am I still under suspicion?"

"Let us say, nobody in the White House Hotel is above suspicion at this present time."

"Fire away," she snapped, "Although I have to tell you Mr Holmes, or should I say Mr Dunwoody, that I shall be making a complaint of harassment against you, as soon as we have regained contact with Guernsey."

"As you wish Madam, but I hope it will not be necessary," he said, "May I ask you just one question? At what point did the Sicilian party purchase your wine for their meal this evening?"

"Some weeks ago," she said, "I advertise online. They're also thinking of importing it to Sicily and the States."

"I see. Very illuminating. Thank you, Madam. You are free to go to your room."

Holmes sensed rather than heard the knife as it catapulted through the air towards them, a sort of a high-pitched thrumming. It passed at speed between Mrs Borger and himself and embedded itself in the wood of the bannister.

Mrs Borger emitted a high-pitched shriek of shock and Holmes stepped forward in case she was inclined to faint. She managed however to regain her composure and said:

"Was that meant for you, or me?"

"I think we can ascertain that quite easily, Mrs Borger," Holmes said, "There is a note attached to the knife."

Holmes pulled the weapon out of the wood and in no time, had detached and unwrapped the note.

"If this does not kill you, Sherlock Holmes, then something else will."

"Have no fear Mrs Borger, the knife was not meant for you. You may go to bed."

The Conservatory Restaurant door was open but there was no-one in sight. From the position and the angle of the knife, it was clear that this was where the knife must have been thrown from. Holmes plucked the knife from the woodwork, screwed up the note and proceeded to clean out the bowl of his pipe with the blade of the knife.

Watson re-appeared.

"Did you ascertain what I asked you?" Holmes enquired.

"I did," Watson said, "Giulio Corionetto booked a hotel in Guernsey some three months ago. He booked the evening meal and overnight stay in Herm the following day."

"And the Strawboulders?"

"Now, they booked a week after the Corionettos. No booking in Guernsey. Directly to Herm for the wine-tasting."

Holmes thought for a moment and then said: "I wonder where the Hotel Manager has stored the bodies."

As if answering some sort of telepathic call, the Manager was standing beside them.

He coughed politely and said:

"Mr Dunwoody, er, Holmes, I have just been informed by one of my staff of something rather disturbing."

Holmes announced, in an almost matter of fact voice:

"One of the bodies has disappeared."

"How did you know?" The Manager's face looked incredulous.

"Which body?" Holmes said urgently, "For God's sake, man, which body?"

"I'm sorry, I don't have that information, Mr Holmes, er Dunwoody. My member of staff didn't say..."

"It's of no consequence. What I can tell you is that Mrs Lucinda Borger's life is in the most terrible danger. Come Mr Manager, I fear we may need a spare key to her room. Watson, bring your service revolver."

"My *what*?"

They all three bound up the stairs together, then discovered that they could make more progress by going up separately.

Holmes arrived first and rattled at the door handle of Room 2. As he had surmised, it was locked. The Hotel Manager fumbled with the keys and unlocked the door. Holmes threw it open.

Mrs Borger was being pinned down on the bed, held round the throat by a strong left hand. The right hand was trying to force the contents of hemlock-infused Californian Blush down her throat straight from a bottle. Mrs Borger was spluttering and choking and frantically trying to resist the lethal concoction.

"Stop! Cease! DESIST!" Holmes cried in his most commanding fashion, advancing on Mrs Borger's attacker, holding in front of him the very knife that had been thrown at him. Reluctantly, the would-be assassin straightened up.

"There Watson," Holmes stated triumphantly, "Is your murderer!"

~

Mabel and Doris got to the lounge early to make sure they had a good seat.

"It's the day-noo-mont!" Mabel explained to Doris, "Usually takes place in the drawing-room but the lounge will do. Have you got your answers written down on your bit of paper? Funny, they usually issue printed slips."

"We forgot to get a drink!" Doris said. "We got good seats but we haven't got a large schooner of sherry."

"Don't worry," Mabel said, "I'll grab hold of a waiter. Oooh, I wish."

~

The assembled company needed no bidding to become silent as Holmes and Watson took centre stage.

Violet Strawboulder and the Widow Corionetto sat on opposite sides of the lounge and staff had been instructed to let them nowhere near each other. They had to make do with long-distance glaring. That said, if glares could kill...

Mrs Lucinda Borger sat at the front, looking pale but composed. She had positioned herself close to Holmes, as if in obeisance to him for saving her life, because there was no doubt, had he been a moment later, she would have been yet another victim of the hemlock poisoning.

Holmes cleared his throat.

"Ladies and gentlemen," he began, "You have been witnesses to the most heinous of crimes and it now falls upon me to reveal the perpetrator of these crimes and to explain to you the circumstances and motivation behind this remarkable chain of events."

"Get on with it," grunted the man with the big military moustache that covered his face.

"First, we have Mr Cephas B. Strawboulder, who died before your very eyes, by drinking a glass of his own wine, which unbeknown to him, was poisoned by a hemlock infusion. Less than an hour later, in the Ship Restaurant, in front of an entire dinner party of Sicilians, Signor Giulio Corionetto is also poisoned by drinking a lethal dose of that same poison. And less than thirty minutes ago, if it had not been for the intervention of Watson and myself with the generous help of the Hotel Manager, a similar fate would have befallen Mrs Borger here."

"Did they do it then?" Mabel uttered in a stage whisper.

"Who?" asked Doris.

"Them two. Holmes and Watson. He seems to know an awful lot about it."

"Doris, he's solved the case. He's now explaining to us what 'appened."

"Oh, I thought I'd got it all wrong."

"Shut up and drink your sherry!"

"So now. Let us consider Cephas B. Strawboulder, a big wine magnate in California. Successful. He controls a large share of the wine trade in Los Angeles. But..."

Holmes held his finger up and broke off for dramatic effect.

"But. He discovers he has a rival. An immigrant from Sicily. Signor Giulio Corionetto."

The Widow Corionetto dabbed a hanky to her eye and uttered a sob. Violet just continued to send inter-ballistic long-distance glares.

"Two rivals in the wine trade. This makes for two enemies. Cephas B. Strawboulder has his rival followed, investigated and discovers that he is making a trip, with his family, to the Channel Islands. To Guernsey, and furthermore that he has booked an overnight trip to Herm Island. So, what does the big Californian Wine magnate do? He too books a trip. With a perfect cover. A wine-tasting weekend at the White House Hotel. What could be better? His aim? To 'deal' with his rival."

Mrs Borger raised her hand. Holmes gave her leave to speak.

"You mean he came here to murder Giulio. Eliminate his rival?"

"I believe so, yes, Madam."

The Widow Corionetto rose to her feet in a fury and had to be restrained before she once again tried to claw the eyes of Violet Strawboulder out of their sockets.

At that point the crowd of onlookers came in with their comments.

"But he didn't, did he?"

"Because somebody got to him and killed him first."

"We were all there. We all saw."

With a flourish of his hand, Holmes silenced them.

"What did we see? We saw a man open a bottle of wine, pour a glass and put it to his lips. Did we see him drink? Did we? Watson, tell the security men we are ready."

Watson slipped out into the garden room and returned followed by...

"Strawboulder!"

It was a somewhat subdued Strawboulder who entered the lounge. He didn't somehow seem as large as he had been. Shoulders bowed, hands tied, he shuffled over to Holmes.

"Perhaps you would enlighten the assembled company as to how you perpetrated the deed, Mr Strawboulder. I refer to your own 'murder'."

Strawboulder didn't speak straight away; it was as if he was gathering his words. He looked at his wife, who stared solemnly back at him, showing absolutely no surprise at his resurrection. Her body language spoke volumes.

"You remember after my little set-to with Mrs Borger here…" He suddenly came to life and addressed the woman he had formerly scorned. "How could you do it? How could sell your wine to that scheming little Sicilian? It's a good wine. We coulda done business together. You coulda bin a contender."

A gasp ran amok amongst the crowd.

"Ah!" Holmes cried, "The truth. This man's tirade against the Kentish wine of Mrs Borger was but a case of…sour grapes. If you will pardon the allusion. But Mr Strawboulder, pray continue with your narrative."

"Well, my shrinking violet went for her walk and I went for my siesta. Tell them what you did on your walk Violet."

"I did what you told me dear. I picked a nice big bunch of cow parsley…"

"Cow parsley?" queried Holmes, "Are you sure, Mrs Strawboulder?"

"Well, Cephas insisted it had to be a particular species of cow parsley. It had to have purple smears on the stem…"

"And that my friends, to someone in the know, as Cephas of course was, is a description of hemlock."

"It didn't smell like cow parsley," the lady said, "It had a smell of…gone-off parsnips."

To a man, every Sicilian in the room, save the Widow Corionetto, rose to their feet, raised their glasses and chorused:

"Gone-off parsneeps!"

"What happened when you got back to Room 3?" Holmes prompted.

"My husband was awake. He seemed to have procured another kettle. I couldn't understand why we needed a second one, but apparently, it was from Room 2 next door."

"You will remember, ladies and gentlemen, that Room 2 is occupied by Mrs Borger. Now here is a startling piece of evidence. Room 2 and Room 3 are connected by a shared double balcony. All Mr Strawboulder had to do was step out on to the balcony and hope that Mrs Borger had left the balcony door to her room unlocked."

"She'd gone to dinner." Strawboulder took up the story. "It was easy. I boiled the hemlock up in her kettle, doctored two bottles of wine and then replaced the whole shenanigans in her room for the chambermaid to find. Easy."

"Shortly afterwards, the charade in the lounge," Homes said, "When I examined this gentleman's body, I could find no trace of hemlock on his lips or teeth. It struck me as strange. But his death was so dramatic, at that time, I presumed he was well and truly dead."

Here, Cephas B regained some of his former composure. His boasts, as always, came easily.

"You're looking at Cephas B. Strawboulder, Actor-Manager of the Liphook Falls Thee-ater Group. My Dastardly Dick was the talk of the town. Violet? Tell them about my Dastardly Dick."

"You got a standing ovation every night dear."

Holmes tutted impatiently.

"The rest of your story please."

"Oh yeah, well. I attached the note to the second bottle of poisoned wine and Violet delivered it to Corionetto by passing it on to one of the unsuspecting Sicilian guests. The rest you know. My 'body' was transported to a spare room in the staff quarters. It took eight of them to lift me and they were panting by the time they got me there. All the Strawboulders have been big people, you know. A die-nasty of giants."

"So, there you have it ladies and gentlemen," Holmes concluded, "This giant of a man, this Strawboulder, this last in the die-nasty, or dynasty as we would know it, stands accused of the murder of Giulio Corionetto and the attempted murder of Mrs Lucinda Borger from Kent. And all because of his greed. He did not want the Sicilian muscling into the Californian wine trade by importing Sicilian wines so he had the man investigated, followed him to the Channel Islands and hence to Herm. On his arrival on the island, he perceives a second threat – that of Mrs Borger, whom he publicly ridicules. So, he fakes his own death in order to dispose of Signor Corionetto without suspicion falling on him. His mistake was to rise from the dead in order to deal with Mrs Borger. Have you anything to say, Mr Strawboulder?"

If Cephas B. Strawboulder did have anything to say, he was to be cruelly cut short of the opportunity.

A knife came whistling through the lounge. Like an aircraft at speed, it seemed to be moving slowly. It hit Cephas B firmly in the chest and he clutched at it with a grunt of pain. Cephas B gave a repeat performance of his death scene, only this time he wasn't acting.

Clutching the dagger, he fell to the floor. Violet got up with a scream. As did nearly everybody else. Guests scrambled for the door to retire to the safety of their rooms. They had had enough murders for one evening.

"Watson, apprehend the phantom knife-thrower immediately. Watson?"

But Watson did not seem to be in evidence. In fact, Watson was noticeable by his absence.

"The deuce! I started off without a Watson, acquired a Watson and now I am Watson-less again."

Then his attention was caught by the note attached to the knife which had eventually done for Cephas B. Strawboulder.

Hurriedly, he detached it and unravelled it. It read:

"Alright Holmes, I didn't get you last time but this should do the trick."

"What devilry is this? It can only mean one thing. MORIARTY!"

Sure enough, struggling his way through the departed crowd, a man approached Holmes with what could only be described as murder in his eyes. He had a black beard and a black moustache and a shockingly thick head of hair.

"Don't tell me you got the wrong island as well, Professor Moriarty?"

The man stopped inches away from Holmes.

"Yes. Sark, wasn't it?"

Holmes leant forward with one hand and stripped the ridiculous black wig off the man. Then with one hand he tore off the man's moustache and with the other, his beard.

"Owww!" howled the man.

"Dr Watson, aka Hercule Poirot, aka Moriarty, aka Reggie Lampwick of Billericay Essex," pronounced Holmes, "What have you got to say for yourself?"

"I didn't mean to kill the big fella," he said, "I didn't mean to kill you either. It was just role play. I missed you both times, didn't I? Just meant to scare you."

The lounge was almost empty.

"Can't you overlook it Dunwoody? I mean, the Yank was a murderer."

"Yes, but we don't put murderers to death in the UK anymore."

"It's alright," came a voice from the floor. "Just a flesh wound. I'm OK."

Cephas B had sat up and was grinning broadly.

"Saved by my silver cigarette cliché. Now, why don't we all have a nice glass of my Californian Blush? *Sans* hemlock!"

~

"Is it over?" Doris asked.

Mabel and Doris were the only two remaining guests in the lounge. A waiter was clearing coffee cups.

"Did we get it right? Did we win?"

"No. Turns out the murder was real. That Civilian fellow. From Sardonica. Or someplace like that."

"Oooh, I don't think that's fair. We ought to complain."

"Shall we go and complain now then?"

"No. Ask that waiter to get us another sherry."

"What a good idea!"

~

ACKNOWLEDGEMENTS

Jonathan Watson (former CEO, Herm Island) – for the encouragement, for reading the stories and for the continuous help and support

'Hidden Treasures of Herm Island' (by the late Katherine Kalamis) – the definitive book of the history of Herm Island and a great source of much factual material that finds its way into the tales. Do buy it and read it. It's incredible!

The Mermaid Tavern – for allowing me to sit for many hours both inside the pub and in the courtyard whilst working on the stories (and for the great variety of good beers).

Hayley James – for her encouraging words about the stories when the going was getting tough. And for the great conversations over Chinese meals at the 'China Red' Guernsey.

Residents of and Visitors to Herm Island – for putting up with my incessant chattering about the book and the stories.

Charlie Fish (at Fictionontheweb.com) – for publishing 'The Herm Miracle' in advance of the publication of 'Where Seagulls Dare'.

James Cassaday (Guernsey author) – for his World War II story suggestion.

Steve Foote – for having faith in the book and all the helpful suggestions and assistance along the way.

Craig Mold – for his brilliant technical help when it came to the re-edits.

The Priaulx Library – for their marvellous collection of books and documents about Herm Island.

Kevin Lajoie for permission to use his aerial view of Rosaire Steps on the front cover, and Visit Guernsey for the photograph of Herm Harbour on the back cover.

Guernsey Literary Festival Committee – for inviting me to be part of the 2018 festival.

Jane Mosse - for spotting all those little errors that nearly slipped through; and for her lovely comments.

Anybody Else – who in any small way contributed to the evolution and production of this book, however great or small.

ABOUT THE AUTHOR

Paul spent most of his working life teaching. Since retirement, his even busier lifestyle means balancing writing with directing plays and musicals. He visits theatre as often as possible, drawing inspiration for his own plays. 'Kilmainham Kids' had its premiere in Welwyn Garden City, in 2017. Other plays include 'The Worst Thing About My Life' which reached the Ovation Awards' finals; this he directed himself using local actors. 'Arsehole at the end of Universe', a modern take on the medieval morality play 'Everyman' was shortlisted for the Alloa Playwriting Competition and went into performance at the Traverse Theatre, Edinburgh. He has also had four horror novellas published.

Paul has been visiting Herm for eighteen years, staying at the White House Hotel. More recently, in the Autumn, he has hired a self-catering cottage, where much of this book was written. "Walking around an almost-deserted island really aids the business of dreaming up weird tales. Likewise, ambling across the Common at dusk allows you to envisage ghostly possibilities."